SEVEN YEAR RICH

TERRY TOLER

Seven Year Rich
Published by: BeHoldings, LLC

Copyright ©2024, **BeHoldings, LLC**
Terry Toler
All Rights Reserved

Book Cover: BeHoldings Publishing
Editor: Jeanne Leach
Contributing Editor: Donna Toler

For information email: terry@terrytoler.com.

Our books can be purchased in bulk for promotional, educational, and business use. Please contact your bookseller or the BeHoldings Publishing Sales department at:sales@terrytoler.com

For booking information email: booking@terrytoler.com.
First U.S. Edition: June, 2024
Printed in the United States of America
ISBN Paperback 978-1-954710-23-8

OTHER BOOKS BY TERRY TOLER

Fiction

Save The Girls

The Ingenue

Saving Sara

Save The Queen

No Girl Left Behind

The Launch

Body Count

Save Me Twice

Powerful Enemies

Deadly Games

Don't Be Careful

Wintervention

Saving Alex

Forsaken

Cliff Hangers: Anna

Cliff Hangers: Mr. & Mrs. Platt

Cliff Hangers: The Quarterback

Cliff Hangers: Macy

Cliff Hangers: Not, Not Guilty

The Blue Rose

Triggers

Seven Year Rich

Noel

The Book Club

The Book Club Murder

The Book Club Rescue

The Longest Day

The Reformation of Mars

The Late, Great Planet Jupiter

The Great Wall of Ven-Us
Saturn: The Eden Experiment
The Mercury Protocols
The Heart of Pluto

Non-Fiction

How to Make More Than a Million Dollars
The Heart Attacked
Seven Years of Promise
Mission Possible
Marriage Made in Heaven
21 Days to Physical Healing
21 Days to Spiritual Fitness
21 Days to Divine Health
21 Days to a Great Marriage
21 Days to Financial Freedom
21 Days to Sharing Your Faith
21 Days to Mission Possible
7 Days to Emotional Freedom
Uncommon Finances
Uncommon Health
Uncommon Marriage
The Jesus Diet
Suddenly Free
Feeling Free

For more information on these books and other resources visit
terrytoler.com.

Thank you for purchasing this novel from best-selling author, Terry Toler. As an additional thank you, Terry wants to give you a free gift.

Sign up for:

Updates
New Releases
Announcements

At terrytoler.com

We'll send you an eBook, *The Book Club*, a Cliff Hangers novella, free of charge.

1

Peach Ridge, Georgia

Rich and Eve were poor but happy.

The day started like any other. Eve got up early to make sure Rich was sent off with breakfast. Powdered eggs and a slice of white toast was the best she could do. They couldn't afford real eggs. Although modest, she made it with love and Rich appreciated it.

He intended to return the favor and stop by the convenience store on the way home from work and buy her some candy. Not a box of chocolates. One bar. A two-dollar candy bar. Her favorite. She'd be touched. Knowing Eve, she'd react like he'd bought her a diamond necklace.

His wife had been craving chocolate ever since they got the news that she was pregnant. A baby on the way only added to Rich's angst. How could they afford another mouth to feed when they could barely afford food for themselves?

Such was the life of a pastor.

Today, Rich felt more like a janitor. He cleaned the toilets and vacuumed the sanctuary carpet. As the church's only employee, he basically did everything. Someone had to do it, and volunteers were hard to come by.

Monday was cleaning day. Most pastors took Mondays off to rest from the busy weekend. Rich had to get in early and get it done. Before the women's prayer group met that night.

He was almost finished. The vacuuming was done, and he was dusting off the organ and piano. It'd been a while since he'd dusted the dark oak attendance board hanging on the wall at the front of the church, so he did that as well.

The "monument" had been in that same sacred spot for nearly a hundred years. Like a shrine. He remembered the uproar when he suggested they take it down.

The numbers were embarrassing.

He stared at the board. Not to see if he had missed a spot, but wondering if there was anything he could do about the numbers.

Register of Attendance and Offering
Attendance Today   36
Attendance Last Sunday   31

He should be happy. Attendance was up.

Offering Today $296
Offering Last Sunday $424

Offerings were down. Some in his church would say the offerings were the most important thing. While he disagreed, the church might have a hard time paying his thousand-dollar-a-month salary if the trend continued.

If they didn't live in the church parsonage, Rich wasn't sure how they would make it.

The last number on the sign warmed his heart.

Attendance A Year Ago   17

They'd come a long way. More than doubled in size. Rich had managed to attract some young couples. One that still attended regularly. For the first time in a long time, they had kids in Sunday School since the couple had three.

When he came to Peach Street Community Church a little over a year ago, the average age of the congregants was eighty-three. The attendance was destined to decrease every year. Rich figured they had about five to ten years and the attendance would be zero.

He had quipped to his wife when she sprung her pregnancy announcement on him, "We can grow the church by one person a year."

She had laughed then but probably wasn't amused now. Her pregnancy was hard. He did everything he could to make things easier for her while trying to keep up with his responsibilities at church.

When he first took on the pastorate, he was twenty-years old and zealous. Determined to win the world for Christ. It hadn't been easy. He married Eve when she graduated high school. They got hitched without her parents' blessing and without their financial help.

Rich wanted to go to Bible college but couldn't afford it. Someday. They were saving up. Although, the saving plan hadn't yet gotten off the ground.

What did he expect? With no degree and no experience, he was thrilled to get the opportunity. When they told him the salary was a thousand dollars a month and they had a free place to live, it felt like they'd won the lottery.

Until they actually had to live on a thousand dollars a month. Then Eve dropped the bombshell that she was pregnant. Now three months along, what should've been the most exciting time of his life was filled with worry. The church couldn't afford health insurance.

What were they going to do?

The doctor said he'd discount his fee. The hospital was looking into some grants. Even then, they were going to owe more than eight thousand dollars.

It might as well be a million dollars.

The hospital said they could make payments.

"How much?" he had asked.

The woman ran some numbers on a calculator.

"Eighty-three dollars a month."

That wasn't bad, but Rich wasn't sure they could even afford that. He asked the church for a raise.

"They're not going to give me a raise," Rich said to Eve last night.

"Even if they don't, God will provide," she said in a determined voice.

He smiled and nodded. His insides churned and still hadn't stopped.

Eve was always so positive. She never complained. Made do with what they had. She cut his hair to save money even though she didn't know what she was doing. She clipped coupons. Cut back everywhere she could. He wasn't sure how she did it. Somehow, she managed the house which was always clean.

"It doesn't cost anything to make the bed in the morning."

He loved her more than ever. He longed for the day when he could give her what she deserved. A thousand times he'd thought about quitting the church and getting a real job.

"God has called you to preach," she insisted. "We have to trust him."

"I can't afford to give you what you deserve."

"I don't care about stuff. I just want to be with you. As long as we have each other, we'll be fine."

Rich dusted off the pulpit. He looked out over the sanctuary. The only place he'd ever preached in his life. He felt like a hypocrite. His messages were on trusting God. Now he was faced with having to practice what he preached.

He fought back the disappointment in himself and started to put things away. The place was so quiet, the sound of a side door opening and closing startled him and echoed through the entire building.

Rich closed the door to the utility closet and went to see who it was.

"I'm in here, Mrs. Ballard," he said, when he heard the familiar voice call his name from the other room. She was probably there to tell him of their decision on his raise.

His heart skipped a beat when he found her in his office sitting in his desk chair.

Mrs. Ballard had been his thorn in the flesh.

Rich was called to the church with a vote of thirty-three to one. He always suspected she had been the lone dissenter. He avoided her like he avoided a tetanus shot. He kept his nose to the grindstone and never complained. Spent most of his time preparing sermons and visiting the hospital and the shut-ins.

Which was why the hospital was willing to work with him on the cost of delivery. They appreciated his work, and it hadn't gone unnoticed. With the state of his congregants, he was there a lot.

"How are you today, Mrs. Ballard?" he asked. He ignored the fact that she was in his chair. He sat down in one of the old side chairs in front of the desk. Yesterday's sermon notes were still on the center of the desk next to his Bible.

"Any day that I'm above ground is a good day. Although . . ."

Here it comes.

"The best thing about dying is that I won't have to listen to any more sermons."

Rich grimaced. He still took things personally. His sermons were getting better, but he knew they weren't great. He had so much to learn.

"Did you not like yesterday's sermon?" He knew better than to ask.

"A little long, wasn't it?"

Another condition of his hiring was that the sermons couldn't be longer than twenty-five minutes. It wasn't really a condition, but it felt like it. He got the message loud and clear. Rich often pushed the envelope and went thirty minutes.

Always careful to finish by eleven thirty, though. So his people could beat the locals to the diner. If he didn't, he might be fired on the spot.

Rich rubbed his nose and tried not to be too obvious. The perfume smell overwhelmed the room. It took all his resolve to keep from gagging.

"How is the misses doing?" Mrs. Ballard asked.

She'll be doing better if you give me that raise.

"She's doing good."

"You mean well," Mrs. Ballard said in her most condescending voice.

"What?"

"You mean that she's doing well."

"That's what I said."

"No, you didn't. You said she was doing good. That's grammatically in-correct."

Mrs. Ballard taught English at the local high school for thirty-five years. Her husband owned the local hardware store until he passed ten years be-fore.

"I'm going to teach you how to talk if it's the last thing I do."

Rich fought down the horrible thought that entered his mind, the one hoping "the last thing" came sooner rather than later.

"About that raise," she said slowly and deliberately for emphasis. "I talked to the deacons about it. As you know, your salary takes up most of the church budget."

Anger erupted inside of him. Rich had already anticipated the answer. Still, he had some hopes which were about to be dashed.

"The church doesn't have much money."

The word was that Mrs. Ballard sat on a nest egg of nearly a half million dollars. The church could afford a reasonable wage if she'd open her pocketbooks a little.

Which made her next words that much more infuriating.

"The church can't afford it right now. We may even have to cut your salary. You saw yesterday's offering. We didn't even bring in three-hundred dollars."

Rich bit his lip to keep from saying what he really wanted to say.

"Maybe if your sermons weren't so long, people would be more inclined to give," she added.

"Maybe if people's hearts were right, they'd give more."

He couldn't help himself. He said it in a rougher tone than he had intended, and she twisted her lips to the side in a disapproving manner.

Rich had never seen the giving records. He didn't want to. He didn't want that to cloud his thinking. He probably couldn't see them anyway. Mrs. Ballard was the treasurer, and by all accounts, controlled the purse strings. Her relatives started the church decades before, and she felt like that entitled her to run things as she saw fit.

Pick your battles, Eve had encouraged him. *At least pick battles you have a chance to win. You'll never win a war with Mrs. Ballard.*

Eve was right. So, a truce had ensued. A cold war so to speak. Rich was polite and mostly took it. But he really needed that raise. This might be a battle worth fighting.

Mrs. Ballard didn't give him the chance to make an argument. She stood to her feet and walked toward the door.

"I'd like to discuss the raise further," Rich said.

"You still have six months before the baby is born. The deacons said they'd reconsider it then."

"We have expenses between now and then to consider."

Mrs. Ballard took her purse off her shoulder. She opened her pocketbook and pulled out a ten-dollar bill and handed it to him.

"Get the misses a little something."

Oh great. I can get her two candy bars now.

What he really wanted to do was hand it back to her. Let her know that he was offended. Instead, he bit his lip for a second time. He only had two dollars in his wallet. He needed that ten-dollar bill.

After she closed the door behind her, he regretted not speaking his mind. He had let her take advantage of him. Again. To get her back, he decided to lock up the church early and go home. Not that she'd ever know, but he'd get some satisfaction from it.

Rich stopped at the convenience store and picked out two chocolate bars. He walked up to the counter to pay.

There was a long line.

"What's going on?" he asked the person in front of him.

"The lottery. Everybody's getting their tickets. Are you buying one?"

"No. I didn't know about it."

"Have you been living under a rock? It's over a billion dollars."

Rich gulped. He'd never heard of such a thing.

"A billion dollars?"

"That's right. I'm buying a hundred dollars' worth."

Rich chuckled. The man might as well flush the hundred dollars down the toilet. Better yet, give it to him. He could really use it.

When he got to the counter, the young girl behind it rang up his candy bars.

"Will there be anything else?" she asked.

The words suddenly came out of his mouth like a hiccup.

"How much is a lottery ticket?"

"Two dollars."

Rich hesitated.

"Give me one," he said.

"I need your numbers."

"How many numbers?"

"Five numbers between 1 and 69."

Rich thought of Eve's birthday.

"Four, eight. Twenty-one." The last number was her age.

"I need two more numbers and a Powerball number."

His birthday. "Five. Sixteen."

"You should choose numbers that are spread out, man," someone behind him said.

The girl glared at the man. "Don't listen to him," she said. "Pick whatever numbers you want. I need one more. Between 1 and 26. The Powerball number."

Their baby was due on the eighteenth.

"I'll go with 18."

She keyed in the numbers and handed him the ticket. He stared at it.

The guy behind him had grown impatient.

"Get out of the line, man."

His heart jumped when he heard another familiar voice. Mrs. Pendergast. Another widow in his church.

If she saw him buy a lottery ticket, she'd certainly tell the deacons.

Rich slipped the piece of paper into his shirt pocket. He hoped she didn't see him.

She did. He stopped when she called out his name.

He made up some excuse and got out of there as fast as possible. Not at all certain why he felt so guilty. Like he'd done something wrong.

2

On the way home from church, Rich decided not to tell Eve he didn't get the raise. Not tonight anyway. Maybe tomorrow. He didn't want to upset her and was determined to make the evening special.

The thought sent a pang of remorse through his heart. That's what it had come down to. A special evening was surprising his wife with two chocolate bars.

Was it always going to be like this?

All of the worried thoughts dissipated as soon as he walked through the door. Eve's face lit up when she saw him. She threw her arms around him and planted a big kiss on his lips.

It never got old. She always made a point to kiss him goodbye and meet him at the door when he came home. The only times she didn't was if she was indisposed. In the shower or bathroom or cooking something in the kitchen.

The affection warmed his heart. As did seeing her. She always looked amazing. It didn't matter how hard her day had been, she went out of her way to make sure she looked presentable when he got home.

Eve wasn't big on fancy hair or a lot of makeup. She was naturally beautiful. In a girl-next-door kind of way. It didn't take much for her to look stunning.

The fact that he was madly in love with her aside, he'd find her attractive if she were wearing a potato sack. Since she was head over heels in love with him and more than willing to show it, her efforts made her even more irresistible.

Today he was getting home early, but it still didn't catch her off guard. She was dressed in stretchy black leggings and a Pensacola Beach Florida tee shirt with the bottom part of the front of the shirt tucked into her waist. Like young people wore it these days.

They went to Pensacola Beach on their honeymoon. If you could call it that. They couldn't afford a hotel, so they slept on the beach with a blanket. When it rained one night, they slept in the car.

The gulf water and a bar of soap became their bathtub. They brushed their teeth in the mornings at the local gas station. A granola bar and soda was breakfast. Which they bought the night before so they could jokingly say they had breakfast in bed.

They couldn't have been happier if they'd stayed in a five-star resort. Maybe more comfortable, but not happier.

"You're home early today," Eve said after several effusive moments, and after she took his hand and led him into the living room.

They sat on the couch. For the first time that day, he felt his shoulders relax.

"I couldn't wait to see my two favorite girls," he said.

Her eyes widened.

"Girls? We don't know if it's a girl or a boy."

"It's a girl. I can tell."

"Whatever it is, he or she has been giving me a lot of trouble today."

She held her stomach and a grimace twisted her lips to the side.

"It's definitely a girl then," he quipped.

She slapped him playfully on the arm. Then leaned back on the sofa. Having him home seemed to lift a burden off her shoulders as well.

"I got something for you," Rich said. He reached into his pants pocket where he had hidden the two bars right before he came through the door.

Her mouth gaped open, and she let out an approving moan.

"My favorites!"

She took them in her hands and clutched them to her chest like she was holding a valuable artifact.

"I wanted you to have them," he said with satisfaction. "Maybe they'll help your stomach."

She rubbed her belly. "They'll help my stomach get bigger. It's already getting big enough."

A running joke between them. They could both stand to put on a few pounds. They'd lost weight since they were married. Neither of them could afford to lose much more. If anything, they needed to put on a few pounds.

Something that wasn't going to happen even if he got that raise.

The tension returned with a vengeance. He tried to tamp it down so his face didn't give it away.

Rich didn't see an end to the financial problems anytime soon. But he wasn't going to let that ruin his mood. Eve sat next to him holding his hand, and all was right in the world. He wouldn't trade her for all the money in the world.

"Thank you for the candy bars," she said sincerely. "That's so sweet. No pun intended." She smiled adoringly as she said it.

His heart melted.

Her perfectly proportioned face didn't have a single line on it, and her skin was as soft and smooth as a fancy sweater. Her eyes did have some slight bags under them from the lack of sleep. The nausea didn't relent even at night.

He'd never tell her that.

Eve's thin reddish-brown hair flowed below her shoulders. It smelled of lavender shampoo. She'd obviously taken a shower not that long ago.

Her head rested on his shoulder.

He suddenly felt self-conscious. Stinky compared to her. The deacons wouldn't allow him to turn on the air conditioning at the church during the week, even in the summer. It was pushing a hundred degrees outside, and he had to do all of the day's maintenance work in what felt like a sauna.

His shirt stuck to his skin in places from the dried sweat. He couldn't wait to get out of his clothes and take a shower. One of the few luxuries of their meager existence. The church paid for the utilities so they could take long showers and baths.

He half expected Mrs. Ballard to complain about the utility bill. So far, she hadn't, so he kept abusing the privilege.

"Are you hungry?" Eve asked.

"Always."

Actually, the hunger pains left him a long time ago. He'd gotten used to the reduced calories.

"You go take a shower," Eve said, suddenly standing. "I'll cook dinner. I have something special for you as well."

"I can't wait to see what it is."

As he walked toward the bedroom door, she added, "Put all your dirty clothes in the hamper, I'm doing laundry tomorrow."

"Will do."

He went into the bedroom, stripped off his clothes and enjoyed a longer-than-usual shower. Even did a rinse and repeat. Normally, he was careful not to use too much shampoo. Even though they bought the cheapest brand on the shelf, he tried not to waste any of it. Taking only a dab and applying it one time.

Today was a day to splurge.

He turned the faucet more to the hot side and basked in the steam. His way of getting back at Mrs. Ballard for not giving him a raise. He'd use a little more hot water out of spite.

Then he felt guilty.

Mrs. Ballard didn't pay the water bill; the church did. If he wasted the water, it came from the tithes and offerings of the people.

Render unto Caesar the things of Caesar. Unto God the things of God.

Jesus's words pierced his conscience. The people gave to God. He was wasting those resources.

Rich turned the water to cool. A good move anyway. The refreshing cold water sent a shock through his system and felt good on his overheated body. He stood with his head down and both arms against the wall and let the icy water penetrate his body. It energized him.

Then he realized he was wasting water and abruptly turned it off.

Would he always feel this guilty? Would they always have to pinch pennies? Ration water? Skimp at every turn?

Rich dried off then threw on a pair of shorts and a tee-shirt and walked out to the kitchen, to a different smell.

Chicken.

He walked over to the stove and lifted the lid. Steam exploded into his nose when he bent down to smell the dish.

Eve slapped his hand.

"It's not ready yet," she said playfully.

"What is it?"

"The store had day-old chicken on sale."

"Chicken breasts?"

"No, silly. We can't afford that. Chicken gizzards and wings. I took the meat off the bones and put them in the rice."

"I smell cheese."

The dish had an orange sauce in it.

She nodded her head.

"I had a coupon for free cheese. I added it to the rice."

She seemed satisfied with herself.

Rich was in her way, and she bumped him aside. The kitchen was small but functional. It had a working refrigerator, an electric stove, and a microwave. Old cabinets that needed painting but were clean.

They thought they had died and gone to heaven when they first moved in. It came fully equipped with dishes and cookware. Glasses and silverware. A luxury they didn't have in their first place.

When they first married, they lived in a trailer. Fifty dollars a week was the rent. Furnished. If you could call the dilapidated pieces of broken-down junk, furniture. The kitchen was bare. Not a single dish or eating utensil. The only thing in the cupboards was one used ceramic coffee cup.

Eve refused to keep it. So, she threw it out, along with the coffeemaker which didn't work anyway.

Nothing in the kitchen worked perfectly. The refrigerator kept things cool, but the freezer was broken. The stove only had two working burners.

"I only use two at a time, anyway," Eve had said. Always looking on the bright side of things.

No microwave. They also didn't have any plates, glasses, or silverware, so they went from yard sale to yard sale until they found some.

One set. Eve scrubbed them like they had nuclear waste on them. He could tell it bothered her to eat on used plates, but she did it anyway after she was satisfied that everything was cleaned to her standards.

The trailer didn't have a dishwasher either. Eve would wash the dishes after each meal.

The parsonage had a dishwasher, but Eve rarely used it.

"I'm the dishwasher," Eve said. "I like to make sure everything's clean."

Rich suspected it was because Eve didn't want to spend the money on dishwashing detergent.

"Dinner's ready," she said.

"I can't wait."

She dished out two bowls of her concoction and sat them on the table which was already set and had two glasses of tap water at each setting.

Rich couldn't remember the last time he had a meal that good.

Actually, he could. When they first started at the church, they received several invitations to lunch after Sunday service. Including one from Mrs. Ballard. He'd never seen so much food. Hams. Turkeys. All kinds of salads and sides. At least two kinds of desserts. Homemade pies. Cakes.

Over time, those invitations dried up. Just as well. Rich was satisfied eating at home. He'd rather be there alone with Eve eating chicken gizzards than having to fake it with Mrs. Ballard.

One time the church did a pounding. Eve didn't know what that was and made a half-hearted joke about it.

"Are they going to hit us?"

Turned out, all the members of the congregation brought them food. Fresh fruits and vegetables. Fresh jars of jam. Some canned foods. Even meat.

It's the only time he saw any generosity from his congregants. Mostly because it had turned into a competition to see who would give them the most food.

He wasn't complaining. They ate well for several weeks. Eve had a knack for making things last.

"This is amazing," Rich said, after taking his first bite.

"Why thank you, kind sir. I'm glad you are enjoying it."

He closed his eyes and savored the moment. Pretended he was sitting at a banquet table. Not wanting to swallow. When he did, the fireworks of flavor lingered in his mouth.

When he finished his second serving, he said, "This big meal is going to make me sleepy."

"Here. Use my napkin."

Eve had a wide smile on her face. He wasn't sure why.

"Nap... kin. Do you get the pun? You said you were sleepy. You need a nap."

He smiled warmly. "I get it."

"Do you want some more?"

"I think I do."

He had a rare third bowl of food. Usually, he tried to save some so they'd have leftovers. Eve did as well. Not since she was eating for two. She'd been better about making sure she got enough calories.

He finished the third dish and before he could do it himself, Eve took the dishes and whisked them away to the sink.

He helped her wash them.

"Do you know why Adam and Eve had the perfect marriage?" Rich said.

"I feel a joke coming on."

"Maybe."

"No. Why did Adam and Eve have the perfect marriage?"

"Because he didn't have to listen to her talk about all the men she could've married, and he couldn't talk about how much better cook his mom was than her."

She smiled broadly. "That's funny. Although, we both know I'm a better cook than your mom."

"That's entirely true."

"I'm glad you like my cooking. It's not much."

They never invited anyone over. Not because Eve was a bad cook. She did the best she could under the circumstances. But because they couldn't spare giving away any of their food.

"Why were Adam and Eve so happy?" Rich asked.

Eve groaned.

"You started it with your napkin joke."

"Why were Adam and Eve so happy?" she asked.

"They didn't have to worry about in-laws."

"I have one," she said excitedly.

The dishes were done, and Eve leaned against the counter with a huge smile on her face.

"God was talking to Adam one day and he told him to go and kiss Eve."

"I wish I could kiss Eve."

"Let me finish. And don't spoil the punchline, mister."

"I won't."

He moved closer to her.

"Adam left and kissed Eve. He came back to God with a huge smile on his face. God told Adam to go and make love to Eve."

Rich felt his heart skip a beat. Making love would be a great end to the evening.

"Adam came back to God with a huge frown on his face."

"Why?"

"He said to God, 'what's a headache?'"

The way she said it caused Rich to laugh out loud. That made her laugh. Then they couldn't stop. They laughed so hard it hurt. Like all the tension inside both of them was released all at once.

After that exchange, Eve said, "I want my candy bar!"

She skipped from the kitchen to the couch like a silly schoolgirl. The bars were on the coffee table in front of the couch.

Eve grabbed one and tore into the package. But she ate it slowly. Savoring every bite.

"You eat the other one," she said.

He wanted to but didn't.

"No. I bought it for you. You eat it."

"Okay. I'll save it for tomorrow."

Eve only ate half of the first bar and put the wrapper back around it.

It hurt his heart. He knew she was saving it as well. He wished she didn't have to do that.

They laid back on the couch and turned on the television. Watched a few reruns of old shows. Fell asleep in each other's arms.

Rich woke up first. The Powerball drawing had just happened, and the television channel was going to commercial. He didn't see the numbers.

It reminded him that the ticket was still in his shirt. In the dirty clothes basket. He would dig it out before he went to bed and check the numbers. Not that it mattered. He didn't win. The odds of winning were something like one in three hundred million.

Eve stirred and kissed him. He kissed her back. She kissed him a little more passionately. A wave of desire went through him.

"Do you want to go in there and make love to me?" she whispered in his ear. "I meant to earlier, but I fell asleep."

"You don't have a headache?" he asked.

"No. And I don't have any nausea either. The chocolate hit the spot. We'd better take advantage of it while we can."

She stood to her feet first, then took his hand and led him into the bedroom.

He forgot all about the lottery ticket.

3

Eve had another surprise for Rich at breakfast the next morning. Cereal with powdered milk and sliced bananas. She didn't usually spend money on what she called "empty" calories. She liked to make things with more substance. The bananas were fine and one of the most inexpensive things you could buy at the store. The sugary cereal was what she didn't like.

"You'll be hungry by midmorning if you have cereal," she had said on more than one occasion.

This morning was an exception. A special treat. They obviously felt the same need to spoil each other. Like he did for her with the candy bars the night before. Either that or cereal was the cheapest option. Finances must really be bad if she had sacrificed health for the budget.

Last night had been amazing, and he felt much better. Even looked forward to getting into the office to prepare his next sermon. Not getting the raise still upset him, but Eve was right. As long as they had each other, they'd be fine.

Eve handed him a sack lunch when he was ready to head out the door.

"It's sliced tomatoes on two pieces of buttered white toast and an apple."

He groaned.

"I know. I'm sorry. Peanut butter is too expensive right now. The drought and all."

Rich had read about it. The long hot period of no rain had decimated the Georgia peanut industry. Pushing up the prices by more than a third. The pain had even reached Peach Ridge. A number of people in the community worked in the nearby processing plant.

He loved it when Eve made him a peanut butter and grape jelly sandwich. The next best thing was peanut butter on an apple.

It didn't matter. He wasn't going to let the meager lunch spoil his upbeat mood.

The best part of the morning was the goodbye kiss. Deep and passionate. A continuation from the night before.

"I had fun last night," Eve said.

"Me too," Rich replied. "If you keep kissing me like that, I'm not going to want to go to work."

One last peck and she said, "Have a great day. I'm proud of you. You're going to be awesome today."

She pushed him out the door, and he left with a warm heart. The Bible was right. Proverbs described a good wife. It said her husband was respected in the marketplace. He was respected. The town had been skeptical at first to an outsider. He'd been winning them over with his hard work and pleasant personality.

Mrs. Ballard aside.

Rich spent the morning working on his Wednesday night Bible study teaching from the book of Acts. He was pleased with the effort although it felt like a waste of time. The same eight would be in attendance. Eve and him. Two widows and two wives who dragged their husbands there to what had become a ritual. They never missed.

The men usually fell asleep. The women frowned when he said something they didn't like. Which was generally more than once a message.

Reading Acts put a longing in his heart. He read about the excitement in the early church when things moved at a fast pace. Three thousand were added to their numbers in one day. Peach Ridge had a population of 2,868. He could reach everyone in town and still fall short of the one-day tally back when the Holy Spirit moved with power.

He longed for that kind of church. With dynamic music. A full house. The thrill of new members walking through the door every day. A line for baptisms.

His church had baptized one person since he'd been there. The wife of the new couple. He'd been shocked when at the end of his sermon, the woman, her husband, and their three children stood from their seats and walked to the front of the church when he gave the invitation.

He dutifully had an invitation at the end of every service. This was the first time anyone had ever responded to it. The couple wanted to join the church, but she'd been sprinkled as a baby. The church doctrine required immersion for membership.

In his mind, that didn't really count as a new convert although he was thrilled to baptize his first person. One of the highlights of his first year of ministry. He couldn't wait to baptize his first real convert.

He longed to see one person saved from his efforts, baptized, then discipled by him. He dreamed of that day. When he could lead someone to the Lord, instead of preaching to the same old people every Sunday and Wednesday.

It'd be nice if Mrs. Ballard got saved.

Rich admonished himself for chuckling out loud at the thought.

As Eve had predicted, Rich was hungry by ten o'clock. He craved something sweet. Probably because of the sugary cereal and the bananas which were high in sugar. His blood sugar had spiked, now he was crashing.

In his wallet was six dollars. He still had four dollars left from Mrs. Ballard's ten-dollar bill along with the two dollars he had before Mrs. Ballard had bestowed her paltry gift on him. Four of the ten dollars had been spent on the two candy bars for Eve and two on the lottery ticket.

That reminded him. He forgot to get the lottery ticket out of his shirt pocket.

A jolt of panic shot through him. Eve said she was doing laundry that morning. If she washed his shirt, the ticket would be ruined.

He thought about calling her, but what difference did it make? He didn't win.

Then he decided to call her. Why waste the two dollars? He might win something. The odds of winning four dollars were one in thirty-eight. Still not good odds, but he could use another four dollars. Maybe he could buy a jar of peanut butter if he put Mrs. Ballard's four dollars with it.

Eve didn't answer. The answering machine picked up. Something the church bought them. The deacons wanted to be able to reach him any time. Day or night.

He didn't leave a message. Eve never bothered to check them anyway. She probably couldn't hear the phone from the laundry room. It wasn't worth driving all the way home and wasting the gas to check on the status of the ticket.

Knowing Eve, she was probably already halfway done with the laundry. He couldn't remember if she did shirts first or shorts and underwear in the first load. Hopefully, she checked the pockets. Probably not. She asked him to do it before he put his clothes in the hamper. Normally he did.

He put the lottery ticket out of his mind. He'd rather spend the gas and time on a trip to the convenience store for a soda. The store had large fountain sodas on sale for 99 cents. That'd still leave three dollars of Mrs. Ballard's money.

Enough to buy a soda every day that week.

The soda would make the tomato sandwich somewhat tolerable. While he should probably skip the soda and save the money, the cravings were strong. He could almost taste the sugary liquid coat his throat and the caffeine would give him a jolt of energy he needed to get through the afternoon.

On the way to the store, he saw a car stopped along the side of the road. A woman stood outside of a late model four door sedan. She seemed distraught.

Did she break down?

He didn't recognize her. She might be passing through or from a nearby town. Peach Ridge was small, but four larger cities were within ten miles of the town in all directions.

Should he stop?

His stomach let out a growl and reminded him he really wanted that soda. A debate raged in his head. The woman probably had a cell phone and could call for help. Although he didn't see one in her hand.

What would he do if he did stop?

Rich knew nothing about repairing cars. He also didn't have a cell phone. Couldn't afford one and the church held a vote and unanimously declined to provide him with one.

"I don't have a cell phone," Mrs. Ballard had said. "And I can afford one. If I don't need one, neither does he."

She still had a rotary dial phone in her kitchen. He'd seen it the one time she invited them over for dinner after church.

Rich didn't argue. He decided he didn't want one. A cell phone would be another way for them to keep tabs on him.

What should he do about the woman?

He passed by and continued down the road. A tug on his heart caused him to slow down. The Holy Spirit nudged him to go back.

At the next driveway, he made a U-turn, and ignored the growl in his stomach. He passed the woman again from the other side of the road.

She was crying.

He did another U-turn and pulled in behind her car. Got out and walked slowly toward her, stopping several feet away so he wouldn't scare her.

The windows in the back seat were down and he noticed two young children strapped in the back seat. Probably no older than four or five. The sun beat down on the car even though it wasn't yet the heat of the day.

The children really shouldn't be in the backseat for very long.

"Do you need help, ma'am?" Rich asked.

She stopped crying and looked at him warily. Like she wondered if she was in danger.

Rich thought the same thing. He'd heard of this kind of scam. A pretty young woman pretended to be broken down on the side of the road. When an unsuspecting victim stopped and offered to help, someone nearby swooped in and robbed the Good Samaritan.

That thought almost caused Rich to laugh out loud. If that was the plan, they were wasting their time. They'd be sorely disappointed. He had six dollars in his pocket.

To him it was like he had a hundred bucks. He might not give it to them. Hopefully, they'd determine that it wasn't worth committing a felony over.

It didn't take long to realize it wasn't a ruse.

"I'm okay," she said, brushing the tears roughly off her cheeks.

"You don't look okay."

She folded her arms and bowed her back.

"I said I'm fine."

He suspected why she was being terse. She didn't trust him.

"I'm a pastor here in town," he said softly. "You can trust me."

She unfolded her arms, and he saw relief wash over her face as her jaw unclenched. "Oh. Thank you. I'm sorry. You can never be too careful."

"It's good to be careful. Tell me how I can help you."

He remained several steps away to give her plenty of space.

She wiped the tears from her eyes. From the redness, it looked like she'd been crying for a while. Something else was bothering her. More than her current predicament. Whatever it was.

"Did your car break down?" he asked. "I'm not good with cars, but I can get someone who is."

She shook her head.

"I ran out of gas."

"That's easy enough to solve. There's a convenience store up the road. Less than two miles from here. I can go get you some."

She started to cry again.

"I don't have any money."

"Do you have a credit card?"

"I do. But they're maxed out."

Now Rich really wondered if this was a scam. The car she drove was better than average. She also wore nice clothes. Maybe she wasn't rich, but she should be able to afford a tank of gas.

"Where are you from?" he asked.

"I'm from Savannah."

Her car faced south. Away from Savannah.

"Where are you headed?"

"To my in-laws' house. They live in Valdosta."

Rich noticed a wedding ring on her finger. A huge rock. That raised even more red flags. Why didn't she have any money? Why were her credit cards maxed out?

Now wasn't the time to question her. The kids were crying in the backseat. She went to check on them.

"We need to get those youngsters out of that car," Rich said. "We can put them in my car, and I can turn on the engine. I know my car doesn't look like much, but the air is cold."

She hesitated.

"Come on. I'll help you."

Rich opened the car door. The woman didn't object. He took one of the girls out of her seat and tried to calm her. The lady opened the door to the other side of the car and took the other girl in her arms.

He carried the girl over to his car and put her in the backseat. Then went around to the front and started the car, turning the air on full blast. The mother put the other girl in the back seat and fastened the seat belts around both of them, then got in the passenger side.

Rich suddenly felt uncomfortable. He hoped one of his nosy widows or deacons didn't see him with a woman in his car who wasn't his wife.

He grimaced inside. To get gas, he'd need a container. The church had what he needed. In the storage shed were two gas containers he used for the lawnmowers. One of his other responsibilities at the church. To mow the lawn when needed.

Could he risk driving to the church with the woman in his car? What if Mrs. Ballard showed up? He dismissed the angst. If anyone saw him, he had a perfectly innocent explanation.

None of their business anyway. Wasn't this the kind of thing they hired him to do?

"I'm going to help you," he said with resolve. "We'll drive over to the church. We have a gas dispenser that I use for the lawnmower. I'll take it to the service station, and I'll get you six dollars' worth of gas. I'm sorry. That's all the money I have. That should be enough to get you to Valdosta."

"I can't take your money."

"You can and you will."

Rich no longer cared about the soda. He simply cared about the woman and her girls.

"What's your name?"

"Edie."

"I'm Rich."

Driving over to the church, she told him her tragic story. Her husband became ill six months ago. He died two weeks ago. They had the funeral in Valdosta.

The illness left them devastated. He couldn't work. They drained their life savings trying to find a cure. Maxed out all their credit cards. Got behind on the payments.

The bank had foreclosed on their house. She sold everything but the kids' beds and toys and her wedding rings to pay for the funeral. She was driving to Valdosta to drop the kids off with the in-laws. They'd give her enough money to go back to Savannah to move everything out of the house.

His heart broke for her.

"Have you or your girls eaten anything today?" he asked.

"No."

They were in the church parking lot now. Fortunately, the storage shed was around the back, and he could park in such a way that his car wasn't visible from the street.

He opened the shed and retrieved the gas dispensers. He went inside the church to his office where he grabbed his lunch and took it back to the car. The woman's eyes widened when he handed her the sack lunch.

He was somewhat embarrassed to give it to her.

"It's not much," he said sheepishly. "But you can have it. There's an apple in there."

"Thank you."

"If you want, I can take you to my house and have my wife cook you a better meal."

"You're too kind. I want to get to Valdosta. Things will be better there."

"I understand."

Rich drove to the convenience store. The place bustled with activity. In the parking lot were several news vans with satellite dishes on the top and call letters painted on the side. A couple of them appeared to be national media which seemed strange.

What would they be doing in Peach Ridge?

Even more puzzling were the two dozen locals who milled around outside the store along with the police presence. Two cruisers were parked to the side and two officers Rich recognized interacted with the locals.

Did something bad happen? Was there a murder? Or a robbery? The police didn't seem to be acting with any sense of urgency.

"What's going on?" Edie asked.

"I don't know."

Rich parked the car and took the dispensers to the gas pump and filled them up with six dollars' worth of gas. After putting the containers in the trunk of his car, he went inside to pay.

The same girl who sold him the lottery ticket the day before was behind the counter.

"What's going on?" he asked.

"The lottery."

"What about it?"

"The drawing was last night. The winning ticket was purchased at this store. Some lucky person is a billionaire."

Rich about fell over as his knees suddenly felt weak.

4

"Some . . . body . . . er . . . won the lottery?" Rich said. His voice quivered as his insides spun like the blades of a box fan.

"Yep. Lucky son of a gun," the girl behind the counter said.

Rich could sense the excitement in her voice and demeanor. Compared to yesterday. Clearly an exciting day for the owner and employees of the store.

If someone in Peach Ridge won the lottery, that'd certainly be the biggest thing to happen in that small town in decades. Maybe ever. The person who won would certainly have a good day.

An eventful day for Rich as well. It wasn't every day that a woman in distress crossed his path. An opportunity for real ministry. Unlike the same-old-same-old.

A thought popped into his head. *What if it was me?*

Rich allowed his hopes to soar for a few seconds. They crashed back to earth when reality hit him as fast as a train speeding through a crossing. The man behind him the day before had purchased a hundred tickets. The place probably sold thousands of tickets.

While the odds were better today than they were yesterday, they were still astronomical. Beyond what his feeble mind could calculate.

"Do you know the winning numbers?" Rich asked meekly. Almost afraid to know. While he had no designs on winning, he already felt the disappointment of losing.

Did he remember his numbers?

Four. Eight. Eve's birthday.

Twenty-One. Her age.

The next numbers were his birthday.

Five. Sixteen.

One other number. He couldn't remember it.

Eighteen.

The baby's due date.

4, 8, 21, 5, 16, 18.

That was the order. He repeated it in his mind several times, so he'd remember them.

The lady behind the counter fumbled around like she was looking for the winning numbers. She lifted the paper in the air with her tattoo laden arm once she found them. Flashed her nicotine-stained teeth and opened her mouth like she was about to read them aloud.

He placed his hands on the counter to steady himself. Took in a deep breath and held it.

"Four," she said, slowly and deliberately. Like an executioner reading a man his death sentence.

His heart did a somersault. That was his first number!

"Five," she added, just as slowly.

His heart sank to the bottom of his stomach. His second number was eight. Five was the fourth number in his order.

"Eight."

His second number was the third number. *Dang. So close.*

If only he had chosen the eight before the five.

His heart accelerated again. Did they have to be in order?

"Sixteen and twenty-one."

Those are my numbers.

He had the right numbers, but in the wrong order. What were the odds someone else picked the same numbers?

The guy behind him.

That dirty dog.

The man heard his numbers and picked the same ones but in the right order.

"The Powerball number is 18," she said.

"I have the Powerball number. Do I win anything?"

"You win four dollars. If you match the Powerball with two numbers, you win seven dollars."

The four was the only number in the right spot. The rest were out of order. Seven dollars would've been a lot better than four. He could buy that jar of peanut butter.

Four dollars was still better than a kick in the ribs.

No one was in line behind him, so he had to ask, "Do the numbers have to be in the correct order?"

"I don't understand the question."

"Do you have to guess the five numbers in order, or do you just have to have the right five numbers?"

"The numbers are drawn randomly."

"I know that." He remembered watching a drawing once. Ping pong balls in a big plastic bin. With numbers on them. Swirling around in the air. He didn't think anything of it at the time. The numbers were displayed on the television screen in the order they were drawn. That's why he figured they had to be in the right order to win.

He rephrased the question. "Do you have to pick the numbers in the same order they're drawn?"

"That'd be impossible. No one could ever do that. As long as you have the five numbers and the Powerball number, then you win the prize. The order doesn't matter."

His whole body went numb. He had the five numbers and the Powerball. Did that mean he won? It didn't seem possible.

What?

Did I really win?

Are you kidding me?

"Are you sure that's how it works?" he asked.

She frowned like it was a dumb question.

"Positive."

That confirmed it. He was the winner of the big prize!

Rich wanted to run through the store like a Pentecostal holy-roller. It took all his self-control to keep from doing so. The lady couldn't know that he had won. The press was outside. The last thing he wanted was for them to start hounding him.

Not until he told Eve.

She'd be shocked out of her mind. *She was going to flip out!* He couldn't wait to get home and tell her.

They could afford a jar of peanut butter every day for the rest of their lives.

Rich was celebrating on the inside while keeping his face as cold as Stone Mountain in Atlanta. This came naturally to him. He had a dry and witty sense of humor. Could tell a joke with a straight face. While his emotions soared, his voice was monotone and his face expressionless.

No way!

I can't believe it!

How is this possible!

What does it mean?

His mind was on overload. He couldn't begin to process all that was happening to him. He could get a new car. They could afford two cars. Brand new. Maybe they should buy used. A car loses forty percent of its value as soon as you drive it off the lot.

You don't have to worry about that anymore, stupid!

He should always be practical. A good steward. This was God's money.

I can finally get Eve a decent wedding ring.

They could pay the hospital bill. Afford medical insurance. The baby could go to college. Maybe he could finish Bible college.

They could get their own cell phone. Was greed already setting in?

What set in were doubts.

Something is wrong.

It's too good to be true.

The elation was overcome by fear. Did he remember the right numbers? He hadn't actually looked at the ticket. Mrs. Pendergast had walked in right as he was leaving. He'd stuck it in his pocket so she wouldn't see it.

So he wouldn't get fired from his church.

Now the cat was out of the bag, they'd know that he had played the lottery. Many people thought playing the lottery was a sin. That's why he hid the ticket.

What difference did it make? He didn't need them now.

That was a horrible thought. Why was he the pastor of the church? For them or for God? He didn't go into ministry for the money.

How would this change his life? Would he still serve God?

The Scriptures flooded his mind like a tsunami overwhelmed a beach village.

The love of money was the root of all evil. It's harder for a camel to walk through the eye of the needle than for a rich man to get into heaven. He who loves money won't be satisfied. A good name is better than riches. Money gotten from ill-gotten gains would never profit.

Was the lottery ill-gotten gain? Mrs. Ballard would certainly think so.

He could see the deacons calling a business meeting right away and firing him on the spot.

Would they? He would tithe on the money. Ten percent would be a small fortune. Maybe they wouldn't fire him. How much was ten percent? He didn't even know how much he had won.

Yesterday, someone mentioned over a billion dollars. His mind couldn't even fathom that kind of wealth.

Was he a billionaire?

He could buy the church building if they tried to fire him.

Then it hit him like a locomotive. He was spending money he didn't have. On cars, rings, church buildings. He didn't actually have the ticket. It was in his shirt pocket.

Oh no! Oh no! Oh no!

He was panicking. Fortunately, the girl behind the counter had looked down or his face would've given away his sudden fear.

What if Eve washed the ticket and destroyed it?

That'd be his luck. He won a billion dollars and lost it because he was careless with the ticket. He'd be the laughingstock of Georgia. Of the United States. Of the world. He'd be a household name for the wrong reason.

Imagine if the press outside the store got ahold of that story.

The church would definitely fire him. For sinning and for his stupidity.

They'd be destitute. He deserved it.

How could I have been so stupid?

Rich tried to dismiss the negative thoughts and muster up his faith and believe the best. He didn't actually know that Eve washed the ticket. Surely, she was smart enough to check his pockets.

He'd be so angry if she didn't. This would be her fault, not his. He felt guilty for even thinking that.

"How much did the person win?" he asked.

"1.6 billion dollars. It's the largest jackpot in lottery history."

He almost fell over. His heart raced so fast, he thought he might have had a heart attack. Right there on the spot. What good would a billion dollars do him if he were dead?

"That's a lot of money," he said casually. "You're right. Somebody is lucky."

"I'd get out of this town faster than a coon chased by a pack of dogs," the girl said in her deepest southern drawl.

A thousand questions flooded his mind at once. He couldn't stop them.

What would they do? Would they stay in Peach Ridge? Would he still work at the church? Live in the parsonage?

"That'll be six dollars and three cents," the girl said, interrupting his thoughts and bringing him back to reality.

"What?"

"For the gas. Six dollars and three cents for the gas."

He almost forgot why he was there.

He turned around and looked outside. The crowd had swelled and seemed to be growing by the minute. The woman and her children were still in his car.

He needed to take her back to her car, fill it with gas, and get home as soon as possible. Preferably without anyone seeing him with her. He had enough worries at the moment without the church accusing him of inappropriate behavior.

Rich pulled out his wallet and emptied it. Six dollars. He handed the girl the money.

"And three cents," she said. "It's six dollars and three cents."

He hadn't stopped the pump in time. Rich reached in his pockets even though he knew he didn't have any coins in them. Then looked around. He was the only one in the store.

"I don't have three cents," he said, embarrassed.

Here he was a billionaire, and he didn't have three pennies in his pocket.

The lady reached over and took three pennies off a tray that sat on the edge of the counter.

"That'll cover it."

"Thanks."

"What do you do if you have the winning ticket?" he asked.

The girl's eyes widened. He knew what she was thinking.

"I don't have the winning ticket. I'm just wondering. I mean . . . I got the Powerball number. Eighteen. I think you said I won four dollars."

"That's right. Bring in the ticket and I'll give you the cash."

"What if I won the big prize?"

He quickly corrected himself.

"I mean . . . what does the person who won the main lottery do with the winning ticket? Does he bring it here? Or she?"

"Oh no. You have to sign the back of the ticket and take it to the lottery office. They'll pay you there. It's a big deal. Especially this one. Being the biggest prize ever."

The biggest bonehead ever. That's what he was. Even if Eve didn't wash the ticket, he was the one who put a billion dollars in his pocket. For all practical purposes that's what happened.

"And I win . . . The person wins 1.6 billion dollars?"

35

"Not exactly. They can take a lump sum payout or take the money in installments over thirty years. I'd take the lump sum. Of course, they take out taxes. I suppose the winner will take home eight hundred million or so."

So, he wasn't a billionaire. Why did he feel relieved? At least he hadn't lost a billion dollars. Only eight hundred million.

He groaned inside.

The door opened and someone entered. Rich decided to get out of there as fast as possible.

"Thank you," he said.

The woman eyed him warily. When he got to the door, he looked back, and she still stared at him. With an accusatory look. She obviously suspected that he had the winning ticket.

Would she keep her mouth shut?

Rich scurried out of the convenience store and made a beeline for his car. Walked right past the crowd and the two police officers. Trying to look inconspicuous. He recognized several people.

For the first time ever, he was glad he only had a couple dozen people coming to his church. Fewer people to recognize him.

Fat chance. Everybody knew everybody. Someone in that crowd knew who he was. They could see it all. Him leaving the convenience store. Getting in the car with someone who wasn't his wife.

Which was worse? The fact that he played the lottery or had a strange woman in his car? Even Mrs. Ballard would have a hard time deciding.

His hand shook when he grasped the wheel. Fortunately, he didn't have to start the car. He'd left it running so Edie and the girls would have air conditioning.

"Are you okay?" Edie asked.

"Why do you ask?"

"You're as white as a sheet. You look like you've seen a ghost."

"I won four dollars at the lottery."

"Oh. Okay. Congratulations. That almost pays you back for the gas you so generously gave to me."

You don't know the half of it.

What would she think if he told her he'd just won a billion dollars?

Not a billion. Eight hundred million.

She'd think he was crazy either way. The thought seemed so wild in his mind, there's no way he could voice it.

"Thanks for giving up your lunch," she said sincerely.

Rich looked in the back seat. The girls were each eating one slice of bread and a piece of apple. It appeared that Edie had given all his sack lunch to the girls.

"You're welcome. I'm sorry it wasn't more."

His stomach growled, reminding him that he didn't have the soda or the lunch. Of course, he was going home immediately. Eve could make him another one. Better yet, they could go to the store and get a jar of peanut butter.

He might eat the whole thing in one sitting. Had the money already changed him? That was a gluttonous thought.

Even if they did win the billion, they couldn't afford to go to the store and buy a jar of peanut butter today. One of the things he forgot to ask was how long it took to get the money.

Assuming Eve hadn't destroyed the ticket. A big assumption.

Of course, if the ticket was intact, he wouldn't leave the house. He'd have to figure out how to guard it.

What if someone broke into their house, killed them, and stole the ticket while they were sleeping?

Maybe they should go into hiding. Where would they go? They couldn't afford a hotel.

He quickly fought back the negative thoughts.

The next few minutes were a blur. He barely remembered emptying the containers into her gas tank or helping her load the girls in the backseat after the car started.

He shook her hand and sent her on her way with his well wishes. She looked at him strangely. His demeanor had obviously changed, and she didn't know why.

As he watched her drive off, his mind immediately turned to getting home and finding that ticket. To confirm he really was a billionaire.

Multi-millionaire.

Whatever.

Guilt flooded his mind as another thought bombarded him.

He should've prayed with the lady. Asked her about her relationship with God. He was in such a rush to get home and talk to Eve that he missed a real opportunity for ministry. One of the few he had.

Not only that, but he also did a U-turn right in the middle of the road. A moving violation in every state of the union. He looked at the speedometer. It read fifty. He was in a thirty-five-mile-an-hour zone. He couldn't force himself to slow down.

I can afford to pay the fine.

The money had already changed him. No doubt about it.

5

Eve loved her life.

Some women might not understand it. She didn't care. Her life, her choice. Staying at home, managing the household, supporting Rich—that's what God had called her to do, and she embraced it.

At first, she was skeptical. Being a pastor's wife had its challenges. Mostly, she hated how mean people were to Rich. She saw his potential. Someday, he was going to be a great preacher. Ministering to thousands. She'd be right there beside him all the way. His biggest cheerleader.

She didn't even mind the struggle. Her grandmother gave her some sage advice when she was a young teenager on the verge of puberty.

"Marriage is not easy. Don't let anyone tell you it is. It's hard. Especially at first. I think every young couple should go through hard times when they first get married," she had said.

Her grandmother lived two blocks over, and Eve spent most of her time there when she wasn't at school.

"When I married Papa," she said, "we couldn't scrape two nickels together. We had to rely on God and each other. That's why we've been married sixty-two years. We didn't have it easy at first. That brought us closer together. Couples that start out with too much don't usually make it."

Her Nana died that year. The words had stuck with her. Every time she counted out change at the grocery store, she thought about her Nana. When she had to put an item back on the shelf, because she didn't have enough money to pay for it, she remembered what her Nana had said.

It's better this way.

Rich and Eve were as close as ever. It seemed like them against the world and that was working. If they could get through these hard times, they could get through anything. She was determined to do everything in her power to make it work.

Today, that included the laundry. Her favorite day of the month. Rich thought she was crazy when she vocalized the words.

"Don't touch the laundry," she had said to him. "That's my job."

"I don't mind helping."

"I want it done right."

They had a bit of an argument about it.

"I can't believe you're getting mad at me because I want to help you do the laundry," he said. "Do you know how many women would love to have their husbands offer to help with the laundry?"

"I can't believe you're getting mad at me because you don't have to do it. Do you know how many men would love to have their wives tell them they don't have to lift a finger when it comes to the laundry?"

She had won that argument. Rich eventually figured out how foolish he was being.

"The only thing I ask is that you check the pockets when you put your clothes in the hamper."

"I can do that."

So, they had an understanding. She basically did everything around the house. All the cooking, dishes, laundry, and cleaning. Rich took out the trash and was responsible for everything outside the house. Mowing the lawn. That sort of thing.

"You make the money," Eve had said. "I'll manage the household."

She could tell it bothered Rich that he didn't make more money for them. It wasn't from lack of effort. He was the hardest working man she knew. Rich wanted to give her nice things. She didn't care. She was happy with what they had.

Like the Bible said. Be content in all things. She was.

This was God's plan for their lives. Nana was right. The struggle would bring them closer. They needed this so they would make it sixty-two years.

"I'll be eighty-three years old," she said out loud when she thought about the prospect of being married to Rich for as long as her Nana and Papa were married.

Eve talked to herself a lot when Rich wasn't home. Some of her best conversations took place when she was alone. Rich was gone a lot. He didn't talk much even when he was home. She had a hard time making friends in that small town. The ladies in the church were much older.

She couldn't really talk to them. In a way, she was supposed to be their spiritual leader. The pastor's wife. They looked at her as a kid. Which she was but didn't appreciate the condescension. They didn't make an effort to socialize with her anyway.

Things would be different when the baby came. Then she'd have someone to talk to all the time.

She did the math. "My baby will be fifty-nine when Rich and I celebrate our sixty-second wedding anniversary."

"Oh, my goodness. I'll be so old."

"Old is twenty years older than what you are," her Nana used to say.

Forty-one did seem old to her.

The washing machine buzzer sounded, signifying another load was ready for the dryer. Eve had allowed herself a few minutes to sit down on the couch. The morning had been busy. She'd made Rich breakfast and prepared a sack lunch and saw him off.

After that, she drank a second cup of coffee, made the bed, washed the dishes, sorted the laundry, and started the first load.

The pregnancy made it harder and was getting more difficult by the day as her belly had started to protrude slightly. Not to mention her energy. Everyone kept telling her the nausea would get better, but so far it hadn't.

When she raised the lid to the washing machine, she let out a gasp.

"Oh, for heaven's sake."

Rich obviously left something in his pocket. The clothes had little pieces of white paper stuck to them. She couldn't tell if it was from a tissue or an actual piece of paper.

"I've told him a hundred times to check his pockets before he puts the clothes in the basket!"

She felt a twinge of annoyance come over her. Not so much anger, but disappointment that he caused her more work.

She blamed herself. "I should've checked the pockets. I know better than to trust him."

Rich had been so good about doing it that she didn't bother checking anymore. It'd been months since this last happened.

"Ugh."

She tried to pull some of the pieces off the clothes, but they were stuck on. Trying to get the paper completely off would take an hour.

Nana had told her what to do.

"Put the clothes in the dryer anyway. With a dryer sheet. That'll get all the lint off."

"Does Papa do that? Leave stuff in his pockets."

"Not anymore. I don't let him touch the laundry. And I always check the pockets."

That's probably why she always insisted on doing the laundry. Her Nana had instilled that same idea in her.

Eve didn't have any dryer sheets. She couldn't afford them. All she could do was stick the clothes in the dryer and hope the lint trap caught it all. She considered running the load twice in the washer to get all the paper off, but that'd be a waste of laundry detergent.

It got on her hands as she transitioned the clothes from the washer to the dryer.

Inside she was fuming.

"How could Rich forget to check?"

"He's a man. That's how."

Part of her defended him. Like it did when the ladies at the church criticized her husband.

"He has a lot on his mind. He's been working hard. I distracted him last night with the sex."

"None of those are good excuses. How hard is it to check the pockets before you put the clothes in the hamper?"

"Not hard at all."

"I'm going to give him a piece of my mind when he gets home."

"I hope the paper wasn't something important."

"That would serve him right."

Running the clothes through the dryer got most of it. She had to shake a few pieces off. To make a point, Eve scraped the remnants from the lint trap and carried them into the kitchen and set them down on the edge of the table. In plain view so Rich would see it when he got home that night.

"I guess I'm going to have to check his pockets from now on. I'm married to a child!"

A conversation with her grandmother made its way into her mind.

"What's the secret of staying married, Nana?"

"Realize that you didn't marry a perfect man."

She didn't understand at the time but did now. She felt the anger dissipating.

"Forgive easily. Don't sweat the small stuff," Nana had added.

Good advice. That's what she needed to do. Rich didn't do it on purpose. He certainly wasn't a perfect man. Even though she was trying, she wasn't a perfect woman either.

"Keep his stomach full and his baby maker happy," Nana had said with a sly grin.

"Nana!"

They laughed so hard her stomach hurt. It made her laugh now thinking about it.

When she remembered her Nana, she always felt better. The woman had practically raised her. She learned nothing from her mother who hated her kids.

Nana was the one who helped her find the Lord. Rich met her right before she died. Before they started dating.

"This one is a keeper," Nana had said to her once they were alone. "Hang on to him."

That's when she started to see Rich in a different light. As somebody she could marry. Too bad Nana didn't live long enough to see them tie the knot.

Eve missed her so much.

The front door opened, startling Eve.

Who's that?

Rich?

Why would he be home so early? Was something wrong? It wasn't even noon.

She walked into the kitchen and found her husband at the table. The pieces of lint were in his hands. A pained expression was on his face. His jaw was clenched so hard, his teeth might fall out.

"That's right, mister," she said roughly, but trying to make sure he knew it was in a playful manner. "You're in a lot of trouble, Buster Brown."

"Oh no! Oh no! Oh no!"

He was kind of overreacting.

His expression was like someone had told him his best friend had just died. Almost to the point of agony. Like he'd been stabbed in the heart.

He clutched the dirty lint and put it against his chest.

"What are you doing?" Eve said. "Now I'm going to have to wash that shirt."

"Tell me this isn't what I think it is."

"It is. You obviously left something in your pocket. It got everywhere."

Rich threw the paper to the floor in disgust.

"Hey! I'm not cleaning that up."

He walked into the living room and fell to the couch. Curled up in a fetal position. She followed him.

"What's going on? Why are you acting this way?"

She couldn't tell, but it sounded like he might be crying. What could be so important to cause this reaction?

"Rich. You're scaring me. What's going on?"

He only moaned. She got angry. Why wouldn't he talk to her? It didn't make sense. She'd never seen him act this way before.

She sat down next to him and put her hand on his shoulder. He *was* crying.

"Did something bad happen at church? Did somebody die?"

Rich sat up and rubbed his eyes roughly. Shook his head from side-to-side and mumbled something under his breath.

"Talk to me."

"Yesterday ..."

He let out another groan.

"What about yesterday?"

"I bought a lottery ticket."

She lurched back. "A lottery ticket! How much did it cost?"

"Two dollars."

She bolted off the couch and stood over him accusingly. "Why would you do that? I scrimp and scrape to make ends meet, and you waste money on a lottery ticket."

"Now's not the time."

"It seems like a good time to me. Is that what you left in your shirt pocket?"

He nodded.

"Serves you right. What were you thinking, spending what little money we have on the lottery? What's gotten into you?"

He didn't answer. Fell back on the couch and buried his head in the couch pillow.

"Why was the ticket in your pocket?"

The doorbell interrupted the conversation. They both jumped.

"Don't answer it," Rich said, as fear washed over his face.

"Don't be ridiculous."

Eve walked to the window and looked outside to see who it was. A white van was parked in front of their house. It looked like a news truck.

The person began to pound on the door. Rich made no effort to answer it.

What's going on?

Eve opened the door when the doorbell rang again. Somewhat annoyed when the person kept ringing it.

She was about to say something harsh when she saw another news truck pull in behind the other one. A person jumped out of the van and ran toward the door with a microphone in her hand. Someone else with a camera on his shoulder came out of the side of the van and sprinted toward her as well.

She slammed the door shut. The person on the other side started to pound on it.

"What's going on? Why are all these news trucks in front of our house?" Rich stood beside her now.

"That's what I've been trying to tell you."

"What is it?"

"I bought a lottery ticket."

"I know. You already said that."

"The lottery ticket was in my shirt pocket."

"I already deduced that. Why was it in your pocket? That seems like a strange place to put it."

"I saw Mrs. Pendergast at the convenience store. She came in right after I bought the ticket. I didn't want her to see it. Some people think buying a lottery ticket is a sin."

"That's ridiculous."

"I know."

"So, I hid the ticket in my pocket. Then forgot about it. You washed it. It's ruined."

That comment struck her the wrong way. A bolt of anger rushed through her mind.

"Are you blaming me?"

"Why didn't you check the pocket before you washed it?"

"Why didn't you check the pocket before you put it in the hamper?"

The pounding on the door got louder. Eve walked over and opened the door and let them have it.

"Quit knocking on my door. If you don't get off our property, I'm going to call the police."

The group on her porch now numbered at least a dozen people. More vans had shown up. The ones with microphones shoved them in her direction. All speaking at once. She couldn't understand what they were saying.

They pressed in. For a moment, Eve thought they might come into the house, so she slammed the door shut and locked it.

None of this made sense. Why was Rich being so evasive? Why were the people on her property? Did Rich commit some kind of crime? Was there an accident?

The phone rang.

"Don't answer it."

"Have you lost your mind?"

Eve walked over and answered the phone.

"Hello."

"Mrs. Martin."

"Speaking."

"This is Woody Dawson."

"Yes Mr. Dawson."

He was a businessman in town.

"Is your husband there?"

Rich was giving her all kinds of hand signals. He used his fingers to make a slashing motion across his throat. Clearly, he didn't want to talk to him.

"He's not available at the moment."

"Could you have him call me? It's urgent."

"Can I tell him what this is about?"

"I need to talk to him about investing in a commercial property I own. I want to develop it into a shopping mall."

"Are you trying to call Rich Martin? The pastor?"

"Yes."

"How much is the investment?"

"Twenty million dollars."

Eve laughed out loud.

"We don't have twenty million dollars."

"I heard from a good source that you do."

She almost dropped the phone.

"I don't know what you're talking about," she said.

"It'd mean a lot to the community of Peach Ridge. I'm the President of the Chamber of Commerce. I'm sure your husband wants to do everything he can for our community. Being the pastor of the church and all."

"Let us get back with you."

Eve hung up the phone slowly. Things started to come together in her mind. The news trucks. The phone call. The lottery ticket. Her husband acting like a lunatic.

She took his hand and walked him over to the couch. Motioned for him to sit down. She was about to demand some answers.

"Was that lottery ticket worth something?" she asked.

"Yes," he said painfully. "It was the winning ticket."

"How much did we win?"

"1.6 billion dollars."

"You're joking."

"I'm dead serious."

She sat there stunned. Not sure what to say.

"Did you say a billion?"

"Yes."

"And the ticket was in your shirt pocket?"

"Yes."

"And I washed it?"

"Yes."

"I washed a shirt worth 1.6 billion dollars."

"Yes."

For some reason, she found it funny and started laughing. Rich wasn't amused.

More pounding on the door. She could tell he was getting angry. His fists were balled like he was ready to fight someone. She held him back.

"What are we going to do now?" she asked.

"I think we have to get out of here."

"Why?"

"Our lives are in danger."

"What are you talking about? Why would our lives be in danger?"

"It just is."

"You're scaring me."

"Think about it. We have a billion-dollar ticket. The press obviously knows we're the winners. Even Mr. Dawson knows. Somebody is going to come to our house and try and take it from us."

"There is no ticket."

"They don't know that."

Eve stood to her feet and walked over to the door. Against Rich's objections.

"What are you doing? Don't do that."

"I'd like to make a statement," Eve said to the group gathered on her doorstep. "There is no ticket. I washed it in the laundry today. It's ruined. We didn't win anything. You can all leave now."

The entire group stood there with their mouths gaped open. In stunned silence.

"Have a good day," Eve said, as she slammed the door behind her.

6

Monday morning
One week later

Rich had called the lottery offices, and they said he had to have possession of the ticket to win. His arguments fell on deaf ears.

"Look at the back of the ticket and it tells you the rules," the man said.

"I wish I could."

"Oh right. The washing machine."

The man on the other end of the phone had already heard the story which was all over the news. Rich could tell he was trying hard not to laugh.

"I'll read it to you," he said. "This ticket is a bearer instrument. Anyone eighteen and over possessing a winning ticket may claim the prize within 365 days from the drawing. This ticket is the only proof of play. This ticket is void if altered."

Running it through the washing machine is definitely altering it.

"So that's that," Rich said to Eve after he hung up the phone.

"He said we could appeal."

"It won't matter. They'll deny it."

They had a good cry and then lived out the worst week of their lives.

Until Sunday.

At least one good thing came out of it.

Rich looked up at the attendance board in the sanctuary and smiled at the reason why the church was such a mess. It was Monday morning, and he was there cleaning it.

Register of Attendance and Offering

Attendance Today 549
Attendance Last Sunday 36
Attendance a year ago 11

Attendance was up.

He laughed out loud. The percentage increase was incalculable. Too bad it wouldn't last. He was skeptical about the number. A member of the press counted how many people were inside and the overflow of people outside and gave Rich the number he put on the board.

That didn't include the number of people who drove up, saw the crowd, couldn't find a parking space, and drove away.

The building didn't hold that many people. They'd brought in every chair available from the Sunday School classes. The choir loft was full. People sat on the floor. Rich was surprised the Fire Marshall didn't show up and shut the whole thing down.

People came from all over. The press interviewed some people who drove from New York to be there. More than a thousand miles. Another person came from Cleveland. Several from Texas.

To hear what the poor preacher would say. To watch a train wreck in progress. Like a good automobile race with a crash.

He looked back at the attendance and offering sign and grimaced.

Offering Today $127

He shook his head. Increased attendance obviously didn't translate into proportional giving. Offerings were down from the week before because the regulars withheld their gifts.

The powers-that-be weren't happy.

They'd come to his house the day everything happened to confront him about the woman in the car. As he feared, someone had seen her. When they arrived and saw all the news trucks in front of their parsonage, that issue was put on the backburner.

The front door was locked, and Rich and Eve weren't answering their door.

Mrs. Ballard had a key and barged in. With two of the deacons with her. Eve was beside herself. "How do you know we were decent?"

"It's the middle of the day."

"This is my house. Don't come in uninvited again."

They ignored her and demanded answers. Condemnation was on the tip of their tongues. Ready to pounce at their slightest misstep.

When Rich told them he bought a lottery ticket and had the winning numbers, they about came unglued.

"You're supposed to be a man of God," Mrs. Ballard said. Her words dripped with disdain. "Why would you give money to the devil's playground?"

"Doesn't matter, anyway."

A certain satisfaction came over their faces when he said they accidentally destroyed the ticket in the washing machine.

"That doesn't change the fact that you bought a lottery ticket!"

Their smirks had turned to vitriol faster than a squirrel can change directions.

"Did any of you buy one?" Eve asked, not hiding her anger. Rich had never seen her this upset. When they didn't answer, she lit into them.

"I saw you," Eve said accusingly, pointing at Mrs. Ballard. "I saw you buy a lottery ticket. A year ago. When we first moved here."

"Why I never!"

She was obviously lying. The gloves were off on both sides.

"This isn't about us," one of the deacons said. "He's the pastor. He's supposed to set an example. What if someone in the community saw him buying a ticket? That makes us all look bad."

"He's a sorry excuse for a preacher," Mrs. Ballard said.

Eve erupted. "He who is without sin! Don't you come into my house throwing stones at my husband. Take the log out of your own eyes before you try to take the speck out of ours."

"Don't use that tone with me, young lady!" Mrs. Ballard said.

Eve threatened to throw them out of the house when they brought up the woman again. An obvious attempt to deflect the question.

Rich calmed his wife and explained the whole situation. The woman broke down along the side of the road. With two young kids. He stopped to help them.

Eve believed him. They didn't.

That made him mad. He stood and walked over to the door.

"Where are you going, young man?" Mrs. Ballard asked. "Don't walk away from me. I demand an explanation."

"I'm going to my car," he replied roughly.

"That's proof enough. You're leaving rather than answering the question. I don't know why you ever married this man. You, of all people, should be upset that your husband is out gallivanting around with another woman."

Eve glared at her.

Rich went out to his car and retrieved the two empty gas containers. Ignored the media frenzy and brought the canisters inside and sat them down right in front of Mrs. Ballard.

"That doesn't prove anything," she said. "Who is this woman? We demand to know. We want to talk to her."

"I don't know who she is or how to get in touch with her. She doesn't live in Peach Ridge."

"What's her name?"

"I don't know."

"You're a liar."

"Edie. Her name is Edie. I don't know her last name."

"I thought you said you didn't know her name."

Eve had had enough. She walked over to the door and opened it. The press swarmed like a horde of yellowjackets. They could probably hear the shouting from outside.

"Get out of my house," Eve said.

"This isn't your house."

"We live here."

"Not for long."

"Get out, please."

"You haven't heard the last of this," Mrs. Ballard said as she walked out the door.

"I'm sure that's true," Eve said.

The only halfway humorous part of the day was watching Mrs. Ballard and the other two deacons navigate through the press.

"No comment," they said to the barrage of questions.

Rich mentioned the woman later that night. "I'm telling the truth," he said.

"I believe you."

He told Eve the woman's entire tragic story even though she didn't need any further explanation. They prayed for Edie and the kids.

Rich thought he wouldn't be able to sleep. He fell into bed exhausted and went right to sleep. Got up early to go work at the church.

He had finished cleaning the sanctuary. That afternoon, he needed to mow the yard. It reminded him that the two containers were empty. He'd have to go and fill them up with gas. He wasn't sure how. He didn't have any money. The church had a petty cash bin, but it was empty.

He half expected the deacons to show up and fire him before yesterday's service. They would if they could. The by-laws required notice before a business meeting could be called to vote to fire a pastor. His fate would be decided on Wednesday evening if the deacons didn't find a loophole sooner than that.

His firing was a foregone conclusion. He only wondered if they would make them leave the parsonage right away. Kicking a pregnant lady to the streets wouldn't be a good look, or so he hoped.

Would they give him a severance package? He prayed they'd at least pay him through the end of the month. He wasn't holding his breath. The firing would be with cause. More than likely the church would issue a statement to the press documenting his moral failures. Fat chance he'd ever get a reference.

The press had camped out at his house overnight. The neighbors on their street were losing patience, and he got glares every time he saw one of them. The media frenzy required twenty-four-hour police presence, which

Rich was grateful for. He was no longer concerned about someone trying to steal the ticket from them. The good thing about the press attention was that everyone knew there was no ticket. And thanks to Eve, knew all the agonizing details. The clip of her standing at the door admitting to washing the ticket had been played on television nonstop for a week.

Still, the press was overzealous, and he was concerned about them invading their private space. It didn't seem like they would leave anytime soon. The rabid reporters pounced on any glimpse of the pitiful couple. They couldn't even open the blinds.

Eve caught a reporter trying to peek in the windows to take pictures of them. Rich nailed sheets to cover the windows until he ran out of them.

A number of the press had followed him to church this morning and were outside the door. Along with a police officer who followed him everywhere he went. For his protection.

Rich decided to clean the pews. Half-heartedly. His mind was on overload. Too many things to process at once.

He came to Mrs. Ballard's pew. The second row on the right. She'd sat in the same seat all her life.

The Sunday service only made her madder. When she arrived at her usual time, someone was in her pew. She had a conniption fit and demanded the man remove himself from her privileged spot.

He refused.

She actually got a police officer who told her he couldn't do anything about it. She had to sit in one of the folding chairs brought in from Sunday School.

One of the highlights of the day in Rich's mind. He smiled thinking about it.

Rich finished cleaning the pews and skipped dusting. He walked up to the pulpit and stood behind it, looking out over the church sanctuary. Remembering. As bad as the week had been, yesterday had been one of the best days of his life.

At first, he was scared out of his wits. He had only dreamed about preaching to that many people. Once he opened his mouth, the words began to flow.

"Turn in your Bibles to Romans 8:28."

He read how God causes all things to work together for good. He shared the details of what had happened the week before. How it made them feel when they realized the ticket was ruined.

"We were devastated."

You could hear a pin drop as he relived the details. The tension in the room was as thick as a morning fog.

He made a few self-deprecating jokes which helped. Deflected all the blame from Eve. It was his fault. He should've checked his pockets.

"My wife says I'm creative. She's right. I've created quite a mess for myself."

As time went on, the crowd warmed to his remarks and people began to relax. He was winning them over. The press surprisingly honored his wishes and didn't take pictures during the service. He told them they could take pictures in the sanctuary before and after the service. He'd gladly accommodate them, and they could get all the pictures they wanted.

"The good news is that I never make the same mistake twice," he said. "The bad news is that I probably won't get a second chance to make this same mistake again."

Everyone laughed.

Well . . . not everyone. Mrs. Ballard sat in her chair with her arms folded and her jaw clenched so tight, Rich thought her teeth might fall out.

"I don't need the money," he said. "I'm already Rich."

That got the biggest laugh and provided a perfect segue into the rest of the sermon. Which went for forty minutes. If he was going to be fired anyway, then he might as well commit the most fireable offense.

Rich read the passage about the rich young ruler who chose money over following Jesus.

The ending was powerful.

"The Bible says not to lay up for yourselves treasures on earth. Things that thieves can steal. Things washing machines can destroy."

The crowd laughed again. Then his tone turned somber. Emotion rose inside of him, and they could feel it. He was on the verge of tears.

"Where your treasure is, there your heart will be also."

Rich paused for effect.

"Do I have regrets? Obviously. Who wouldn't? Do I feel like a fool? Yes. Do I feel like I let down my wife? That's the worst ... part."

His voice cracked. A tear escaped out of his eye and ran down his cheek. He didn't bother to brush it away. He couldn't look at Eve or he would completely lose it.

"I do feel like an idiot. But I'm only human. I did something really stupid. I can't even believe how stupid it was."

More tears escaped, and he paused to wipe them away.

His voice softened to barely above a whisper. "But I already consider myself rich. No pun intended this time. I have the most amazing woman in the world. My wife, Eve. She never accused me. Never blamed me. She said she would stand by me no matter what. For richer or for poorer. It looks like we're going to be poorer for a while longer, honey. I'm sorry."

Eve clutched a tissue. Fought back her own tears.

"Dear, would you come and stand by me?"

She did so reluctantly. The crowd gave her an ovation. Everyone clapped except Mrs. Ballard and the deacons.

He put his arm around her. "I love this woman so much. I wouldn't trade her for ten billion dollars."

More applause. This was the first time he'd heard clapping in the church. It was frowned upon.

"This will probably be the last sermon I preach at this church."

"Amen," Mrs. Ballard said.

A groan went through the congregation. Then murmuring. He'd given the press a headline.

"That's okay. My faith is strong. Our faith is strong."

He asked Eve to go to the piano and play the hymn *I Surrender All*. She started playing softly. He'd never heard her play so beautifully.

Rich could feel the anointing upon him.

"I believe Romans 8:28. I don't know why this happened to us, but I believe God will work this thing for our good. Do you want to know why?"

He shared with them how he came to know the Lord. Why he trusted him with his life. Talked about how to get saved.

Then gave an invitation. He asked people to close their eyes. More than a dozen people raised their hands to accept Christ. Dozens more raised their hands seeking to rededicate their lives.

It seemed like God really was working things together for good. If he had to lose a billion dollars for a dozen people to get saved, then he was glad the washing machine destroyed the ticket.

Rich and Eve posed for pictures after the service ended but didn't comment. Their attorney had told them not to.

At least a dozen lawyers had called and left a message on their answering machine offering their services. One gave them the idea to hire an attorney.

"I'll do it on a contingency," the man said. "It won't cost you anything out of pocket. I'll take forty percent of the amount of money once I secure it for you."

"I bet he would," Rich said, with a mocking laugh.

"We should hire an attorney," Eve said.

"We don't have any money."

"God will provide."

And he did. A local lawyer agreed to take the case pro bono. He did it for the publicity, but they didn't care. Paul Jackson had been on television nonstop advocating for his clients. He argued that a public outrage would help their case.

The nation was riveted by their story. It hadn't died down even after a week. If anything, the story had gained legs. The few times they turned on the television, it didn't take long to find a station talking about them. Every talk show, news show, gossip columnist, blogger, and coffee cooler break room were talking about Rich and Eve Martin.

The couple who lost 1.6 billion dollars. They even made the national news with daily updates.

The nation was divided. Half blamed her; half blamed him. Half believed they should get the money; half felt like the rules were the rules.

Even if they didn't get the lottery money, it looked like they might get a financial windfall out of it. They'd had a number of offers already. People had left messages on their answering machine. A number of them had contacted their attorney. They'd been offered book deals. Movie deals. Networks were in a bidding war to get the first interview with them.

Paul Jackson was sorting through it all.

He felt like they should wait until they heard from the appeal before deciding anything. Which should come at any time.

Jackson secured video footage from the convenience store showing Rich purchasing the ticket. Lottery records confirmed the date and time the winning ticket was purchased. There's no doubt about what happened.

The incontrovertible evidence was plastered all over the news. A groundswell of support for them was growing.

Jackson wasn't optimistic. The rules of the lottery were clear. The explanation had gone over his head.

It seemed so unfair.

"Why should the lottery get to keep all that money?" Eve had asked.

"They don't get to keep it. It goes into an education fund."

"That'd be a good thing," Eve said. "At least it'll be put to good use."

Rich heard a commotion outside the church. It startled him. He opened the door. Jackson was making a statement to the press.

"Earlier today, the Lottery Commission denied my client's appeal. This is a travesty of justice."

"What are you going to do now?" a reporter asked.

"Later today, I'm filing a lawsuit against the Lottery Commission demanding justice for my clients. We're filing a motion for an emergency hearing."

"What do you hope to accomplish?"

"We hope a judge will award the winnings to my clients. They deserve it."

They had talked about it. Rich knew this would be the next step if the appeal was denied.

The lawsuit was their last hope.

7

Ten days later

The courtroom was smaller than the church sanctuary, but more people than it held tried to get into it. For the biggest trial the county, maybe the state of Georgia, had ever seen.

More than two thousand people had registered for fifty-four of the coveted seats. Ironically enough, the lucky few were chosen by lottery. When the Bailiff announced the winners and handed out tickets, he jokingly said, "Be sure you don't leave the ticket in your shirt pocket and put it through the washer. You won't be able to get in if you don't have it."

Rich sat nervously at the plaintiff's table with his attorney, Paul Jackson. Eve wasn't allowed to sit there. Technically, she wasn't a party to the lawsuit. Rich purchased the ticket and was the rightful owner. She had rights as a spouse, but not necessarily to sue the Lottery Commission.

She could be called to testify, but Jackson didn't think either of them would end up on the stand at this hearing. This was a motion for emergency relief. To win they had to show a cause of action that they were likely to win on the merits and convince the judge of the urgent nature of the request and that they'd suffer irreparable harm if he didn't intervene.

An uphill battle on both counts.

Eve was given one of the seats right behind the plaintiff's table. She'd joked about selling it to the press so she could have enough money to buy some groceries. Rumor had it some people sold their seats to the press for up to five thousand dollars.

They sat on the right side of the courtroom facing the bench. Paul Jackson had gotten there early. He said he always wanted to be on the right side of the law. Both legally and literally.

Privately, he had tried to temper their expectations. He wasn't sure they could win on the merits or prove an emergency existed. The rules of the lottery were clear. To win, a perfectly intact ticket with the winning numbers had to be presented to the Lottery Commission within three hundred and sixty-five days of the drawing.

Something Rich couldn't do. The rules had no provision for lost or stolen tickets.

Jackson would make his best arguments. The language on the back of the ticket was problematic.

A validated ticket is the only proof of play. Submission of a winning ticket is the only way to claim a prize.

Of course, Rich never read the back of the ticket which was no defense. Additional language was even more conclusive.

All printing on the ticket shall be present in its entirety and be legible.
The ticket shall be intact.
The ticket shall not be mutilated, altered, or tampered with in any manner.
The Commission is not responsible for lost tickets.

"We're going to lose," Rich had said.

"If this were before a jury, we'd win a hundred out of a hundred times," Jackson had said. "In front of a judge, you never know. He'll need a compelling reason to override the rules of the Lottery Commission."

A throng of Lottery Commission attorneys sat at the other table. Rich counted six of them in designer suits. Paul Jackson said they had three more who weren't allowed in. Not enough room. The judge had been annoyed in the pretrial conference that so many attorneys were in his office.

The lead attorney, Howard Dunn, a slick, smooth-talking, monogrammed shirt with cufflinks—a thousand-dollar-an-hour type—came over and introduced himself to Rich and Eve. Almost apologetically.

"I hope you win today," he said. "If it were up to me, you would."

"Can I tell the judge that?" Paul Jackson quipped. "We can make a joint motion that defendants no longer dispute our claim."

"Nice try, Counselor. Sorry though. I have a job to do. If we didn't oppose this, you can imagine the can of worms we'd open up. As it is, more than five hundred people called the offices over the last few days claiming to have the winning ticket. Some say they lost it. One guy said your client stole it from him. A few claimed they put it through their washing machine."

"We all know that Mr. Martin is the one who purchased the real one," Paul Jackson said.

"We still have to investigate every claim."

"That shouldn't be hard. Mr. Martin is on videotape purchasing the ticket."

Mr. Dunn held his hands in the air in surrender. "We aren't disputing it."

"Then pay my clients what they deserve."

"Let's save the arguments for the judge, shall we?"

"That's what we intend to do."

"Good luck."

"We're ready."

Paul Jackson had a chip on his shoulder. He seemed to relish the opportunity to go up against the high-powered lawyers.

"It feels like it's us against the world," Rich said. "Like you said, the odds aren't in our favor."

When pressed, Jackson gave us a ten percent chance.

"I'd like to smack that smug look off Dunn's face," Jackson whispered to Rich.

Rich didn't mind the bravado. He was glad to have a fighter in his corner.

"The one thing we have going for us is that this judge is from this county. He grew up here. He knows what winning the lottery could do for this area. The notoriety is worth millions in advertising. Not to mention the money that could be invested in the community. I'm going to make the argument that you're staying here."

"That's fine," Rich said. "Although we haven't decided."

For now, they were still in the parsonage even though he had been fired from his job at the church. In a close vote. 17-16. They hadn't been given a move-out demand letter. Not yet anyway.

Rich heard that Mrs. Ballard had tried to get one of the seats in the courtroom but didn't win the lottery. She was on the plaintiff's witness list, although Jackson didn't think she'd ever make it to the stand. He would object based on relevance. He doubted the judge would let her testify or that they'd even call her.

"What does your potential affair with a woman have to do with whether or not you deserve the proceeds from the lottery ticket?" Jackson had said.

"My husband didn't have an affair," Eve said angrily.

"I know," Jackson said. "I'm just saying it's irrelevant."

"It's irrelevant because it never happened," Eve said, holding back the tears.

"I don't disagree. Your husband's character is irrelevant to these procedures."

"I'll put my husband's character up against anyone's."

"Like I said, I don't think any of this will come up. This is an evidentiary hearing. The judge will only want to hear the facts. He already knows them through the motion and their response."

That conversation took place before they entered the courtroom. In his office before they rode over together. Remembering only added to Rich's anxiety.

A door opened, and the bailiff entered the courtroom sending Rich's heart doing laps around his chest. He felt like he wanted to throw up.

"All rise," the bailiff said. "This court is now in session with the honorable Judge Mannasah Corbett presiding."

Rich thought that was a bad sign. Manasseh was a wicked king in the Bible. He became king at twelve years old. His father, Hezekiah, was a good king of Israel and had destroyed the idols to Baal and foreign gods. Manasseh reversed those reforms, and the Bible said he committed personal sins and killed many innocent people.

Eve pointed out that this judge spelled his name differently than the biblical king. Jackson had defended the judge. Said he had a good reputation for being fair. None of that got rid of Rich's anxiety.

Really, he mostly wanted the whole thing to be over. Not likely to happen. The only way was for them to win. In that case, the Lottery Commission probably wouldn't appeal. If they lost, then it could be tied up on appeals for years.

"You may be seated," the judge said, the pounding gavel drowned out his words.

Corbett was older, evident by his thinning white hair. His eyes were small behind oval glasses. His mouth was set in a determined straight line.

Jackson said not to let the conservative looks deceive them. Corbett was unconventional. He ran his courtroom by the seat of his pants. Often grandstanding as much as the attorneys. He allowed a wild west mentality. Gave the attorneys the opportunity to mix it up. He often joined in the fray. He'd retire soon and didn't have anything to lose and was rarely overturned on appeal, so he made confident and bold decisions.

Jackson wasn't sure how the judge would handle today since there were cameras in the courtroom. This was unchartered territory for all of them. The feed was transmitted live across the world. The judge had demanded that the cameras not show the plaintiffs unless they were called to the stand. To protect their privacy.

As if Rich and Eve had any privacy left to protect. The entire world knew who they were and everything about them. Even the situation with Edie. Conveniently brought up at his firing and leaked to the press. So far, the zealous reporters hadn't figured out who she was. Rich hoped she would escape their scrutiny. She had enough to deal with already.

After a few formalities, Judge Corbett said, "Mr. Jackson, you have the floor. This is your rodeo. I've read your complaint. Please don't tell me anything I already know."

Jackson stood to his feet. Rich could see his lawyer's hand shaking as he carried his notes to the podium.

"Thank you, Your Honor. I'll be brief."

"I appreciate it."

"The facts are not in dispute. My client, Rich Martin, purchased a lottery ticket on June sixth at the *Grab It and Go* convenience store in Peach Ridge, Georgia. Turns out, that ticket has the winning number to that week's Powerball drawing. I believe that counsel for the defense will stipulate that Mr. Martin did indeed purchase the winning ticket."

Howard Dunn stood to his feet and said, "That does appear to be the case, Your Honor, but we are not ready to stipulate to that fact."

"It appears to be or is the case?" the judge said tersely.

"We have seen footage from the convenience store, showing Mr. Martin purchasing a lottery ticket around the time that the winning ticket was purchased. The Commission ran a transaction file report and checked the numbers listed in the report by the numbers printed out by the computer in the convenience store. The transaction file showed the sequence of numbers were purchased around the same date and time as the time stamp on the convenience store video cameras."

"Not around the time," Jackson interrupted. "At the exact time."

"Was it the exact time?" the judge asked.

"That appears to be the case, Your Honor," Dunn said.

The judge seemed irritated. Rich could see what Jackson meant about the judge. He clearly didn't like the verbal gymnastics by the defendant's attorney. Why didn't Dunn just admit publicly what he had admitted privately?

"It is the case," Jackson said. "We have incontrovertible evidence that Rich Martin is the person who purchased the ticket. Those are also his numbers. His wife's birthday is April eighth. Four eight. His birthday is May sixteen. Five, sixteen. His wife is twenty-one years old and eighteen is the baby's due date. Those were the numbers Mr. Martin picked, and those were the winning numbers."

"We haven't actually seen the ticket," Howard Dunn said, interrupting again. "I'm not trying to be evasive, but the lottery rules require that the winner present the ticket to the lottery office and sign the back of the ticket. Mr. Martin has not done so."

"He can't, Your Honor."

Dunn pounced. "Plaintiff admits that he does not have possession of the ticket and he did not sign the back of the ticket as required by the rules and regulations. Therefore, he is not the bearer or holder of the ticket. As such, he is not entitled to payment of the lottery prize. My client was well within its rights to deny the claim."

"What if the ticket was stolen from him?" Jackson said. "In that instance, he wouldn't be the holder of the ticket either. Are you arguing that he wouldn't have the legal right to the prize if he were the one who purchased the ticket, and someone stood outside the lottery offices and stole it from him as he was entering?"

"We don't deal in hypotheticals in my courtroom," Judge Corbett said.

We're going to lose.

Eve stood from her seat and walked toward Paul Jackson and got his attention. Catching everyone by surprise, including the judge who struck his gavel. Rich wasn't sure what to do, so he remained seated.

"Excuse me, Your Honor," Jackson said. "May I have a second to confer with my client."

"Make it quick."

A minute or so later, he said, "Your Honor, my client does have the ticket."

A murmur went through the courtroom. The judge gaveled them down.

"You have the ticket?" the judge asked.

Howard Dunn's eyes widened in surprise. The multiple attorneys at the defense table scrambled, going through their papers.

"Yes, Your Honor. Eve Martin has it in her purse."

"Well, let's see it then," the judge said.

Dunn stood to his feet. "Objection. Foundation."

Jackson responded before the judge could rule on the motion.

"Your Honor, I'd like to call Eve Martin to the stand."

"That sounds like a good idea. Go ahead."

Jackson swung the gate open, and Eve walked forward stopping directly in front of the witness stand where the bailiff stood with a Bible.

"Raise your right hand and put your left hand on the Bible. Do you swear to tell the truth, the whole truth and nothing but the truth, so help you God?" he said.

"I do."

Paul Jackson went through a few formalities. State your name. Your relationship with the plaintiff. Those kinds of questions.

"Mrs. Martin, do you have the winning ticket in your possession?" he asked.

"Yes. It's in my purse. Would you like for me to get it for you?"

The murmuring started again in the crowd. Only louder this time. The judge pounded the gavel, then issued a warning.

"I can get it for you."

"Yes, please."

The judge leaned forward from the bench. The defendant's attorneys sat on the edge of their seats.

Eve opened her handbag and pulled the scraps of what was left of the ticket and cupped them in her hands.

"This is the ticket. What's left of it anyway."

A roar of laughter went through the crowd.

"Why is the ticket shredded?" the judge asked, even though he knew the answer. Unless he'd been living under a rock for the last ten days or hadn't actually read the complaint.

Jackson answered for her. "The videotape at the convenience store shows Mr. Martin purchased the ticket and then put it in his shirt pocket."

"What happened to the ticket?" the judge asked Eve in a soft tone.

"I ran it through the washing machine," she said with a pained expression.

She was adorable. Even the judge smiled in sympathy for her.

"Silly me. I do the laundry. My husband put his shirt in the hamper."

She looked at the judge when she said it. "He didn't take the ticket out before he put it in the clothes hamper. I should've checked the pockets, but I didn't. I didn't even know he bought a lottery ticket."

Mr. Dunn stood to his feet again. "The rules of the lottery clearly state that for a ticket to be valid it must be intact. This ticket is unrecognizable."

"I've read the rules on the back of the ticket," the judge said, clearly annoyed by the interruption.

"Your Honor, I'd like to enter the remains of the ticket as plaintiff's exhibit 1," Jackson said.

"I object, Your Honor. Plaintiff has not presented any proof that this is the winning lottery ticket."

"It's the ticket," Eve said.

"Like I said, there's no proof."

She took one of the pieces in her hand. "I found this piece this morning in my husband's shirt pocket. This small remnant has the Powerball number on it. Number 18 is showing. You can see the logo on the ticket. Eighteen is my baby's due date."

She held the tiny piece in the air even though no one in the room but her could see the number.

"Your Honor, we need the opportunity to inspect this ticket for authenticity," Dunn said.

"Does it really matter?" the judge retorted. "You've already stipulated that Mr. Martin purchased the ticket. Mrs. Martin testified that she found this remnant in his shirt pocket. She admitted washing it. Do you really want to dispute those facts?"

Dunn ratcheted up the pressure. Creating more intensity behind his argument.

"I would remind the court that the plaintiff was notified on the back of the ticket that he was required to follow the rules and regulations of the lottery and that the ticket was proof of play. He has failed to comply with the procedures necessary to claim the prize. One of which is that he has not signed the back of the ticket."

Jackson responded. "In Canada and the UK, if you lose a ticket or it is destroyed for some reason, you can file a claim within thirty days. If you can prove that you did indeed purchase the ticket, then you can claim the prize."

"Do I need to remind counsel that we live in the United States of America?" Dunn said. "Not Canada or Great Britain."

"I've heard enough," the judge said. "I'm ready to make my ruling. You may step down Mrs. Martin. Thank you."

It all happened so fast. Eve didn't know what to do. The attorneys seemed surprised as well. After prodding from Jackson, she closed her purse and left the remnants of the ticket still lying on the ledge of the witness stand.

Paul Jackson waited for Eve to walk past him before sitting down, then he returned to the plaintiff's table and sat next to Rich.

The judge waited for everything to settle down before beginning his ruling.

We're going to lose.

8

The judge said he was ready to rule.

Rich's heart was beating so hard, he could hear it in his ears. His clammy hands were clasped together under the table so no one could see them shaking.

He feared the worst. The judge didn't seem at all sympathetic to their case. Rich heard the facts. They were straight forward. The ticket was not intact. Only one number was visible. The rest were unrecognizable.

While it seemed unfair, the rules were the rules.

Rich watched his wife walk from the witness stand back to her chair. His heart was warm with admiration. He admired her courage for standing up and testifying.

He didn't know about the remnants of the ticket in her purse until that morning when she mentioned it to him.

"I kept all the scraps. I thought we might need it for evidence," she had said.

"Good thinking."

"It's been in my purse all this time."

"Bring it with you to court."

"I have an idea," she said out of the blue. She left the room and came back a few seconds later.

"I found this in your pocket," she said, holding the fragment in her hand.

They were both amazed the number eighteen was still intact.

"This might mean something," Rich said. "Bring it as well."

They had meant to tell Jackson but didn't get the chance. Things were a whirlwind before the hearing, and Jackson spent most of his time back in the judge's chambers. Rich forgot about it until he saw Eve stand and interrupt him in the middle of the hearing.

Not that it would make a difference. It didn't change the fact that most of the ticket had been destroyed.

The judge had his head down. He began speaking in a slow, monotone voice. A different cadence and key. Obviously, his pontificating voice. The crowd was so quiet, Rich could hear the sound of a train going through the center of town.

"On the surface, this is a fairly straightforward case," Judge Corbett said. "I find the plaintiff's action against the Lottery based on breach of contract is lacking. If anything, the plaintiff has failed to fulfill his end of the agreement by not following the rules and regulations of the lottery which are clearly spelled out on the back of the ticket."

Rich's heart had been beating faster than a speeding bullet, but it now sank to the bottom of his chest. It seemed to lose all its power and enthusiasm and beat so slowly he thought he might faint.

"Plaintiff's second claim states that the lottery's actions are arbitrary or capricious. Plaintiff makes the argument that the state of Georgia has paid prizes for damaged tickets in the past. While that's true, it's been limited and only for instant prizes under a thousand dollars. This prize is much larger. It would stand to reason that the Lottery should take greater care in administering a prize worth 1.6 billion dollars."

That makes sense.

"The Lottery has a fiduciary responsibility to ensure the public that the rules of the game are followed and that the prize is awarded to the correct person. The circumstances in this case make it much harder for them to do so."

Guilt flooded Rich's emotions and caused his breathing to speed up. He wanted to blame himself again. But he'd kicked himself in the rear so many times, he didn't have the mental energy to do it again.

"How are they supposed to do that without a ticket?" the judge asked. He looked up at the ceiling like he was deep in thought.

"I suppose, it's instructive that no other winner has emerged with the winning ticket even though we know someone won."

Yeah. Me.

No other winner emerged because I won.

Hopefully, that's what the judge meant.

"We do have the video evidence. Mr. Martin was present at the exact date and time when the winning ticket was purchased. Mr. Jackson provided the meaning behind the numbers providing some circumstantial proof that those were the ones Mr. Martin chose. I found Mrs. Martin's testimony moving. It's heartbreaking that the ticket was destroyed. I feel for them. I'm sure they both have been beating themselves up over it. I'm genuinely sorry this has happened to you."

The judge gazed directly at Rich.

Rich was moved by the sentiment. Cameras were rolling, but it seemed sincere.

"Mrs. Martin had in her possession the remnants of the ticket. I'm convinced that is indeed the winning ticket. The Powerball winning number present on the fragment is conclusive in my mind."

The pile of shredded paper still sat on the witness stand. A reminder to them all.

"This court is convinced without any doubt that Mr. Martin purchased the winning ticket."

Thank you.

Judge Corbett looked down at his notes.

"As I mentioned earlier, it's also true that the Georgia State Lottery Commission has paid out prize money for damaged tickets in the past. The plaintiffs pointed this out in their brief. The argument is informative. Two hundred and twenty-five times, a prize has been paid out based on a mutilated ticket. None has been paid out for lost tickets. None for prizes over a thousand dollars."

The judge was hard to read. He went back and forth. At first it seemed like he was siding with the defense. Then with the plaintiffs. Then the defense. Like watching a tennis ball go back and forth across a net.

Get to it. Please.

"For much of the hearing, I was inclined to side with the defendant. I considered this a lost ticket. The state of Georgia has never paid out prize money for lost tickets."

And?

"Now I consider this a mutilated ticket. Thanks to Mrs. Martin. She has presented to this court evidence beyond the plaintiff's word that the ticket destroyed in the washing machine is indeed the winning ticket. I find it credible considering the number eighteen is clearly visible on the remnants of the ticket and you can even see a part of the lottery logo on the paper."

You said that already. Does it mean we win?

"Even though the Lottery has paid out winnings in the past for a mutilated ticket, that's not enough to rule in plaintiff's favor."

Make up your mind.

The judge was driving him crazy. Going back and forth. He had no idea how he was going to rule.

"So, I must decide if the Lottery is being arbitrary, capricious, or discriminatory by denying the plaintiff's claim. The Lottery should explain to Mr. Martin why his claim is different than the others. Size of the prize is not reason enough in my mind."

I agree.

"Nevertheless, the burden of proof is on the plaintiff. Their argument falls short. I don't find that the plaintiff has provided evidence that the lottery's failure to pay his claim is arbitrary, capricious, or discriminatory. This policy seems to be consistent for larger prizes and would apply to anyone making the same claim under the same circumstances. Mr. Martin has not been singled out in any way."

This is torture.

"Furthermore, we do not live in Canada or the United Kingdom. We fought a war more than two hundred years ago so that we would not have to live under the laws of England. I don't really care what they do in their lottery, and counselor for the defense should not have made that argument in my courtroom. If he wants to practice law in Canada or Great Britain, then that's what he should do."

He hates us.

"However . . ."

Rich's heart did a backflip. What did that mean? *However?*

"The United States of America has formed a more perfect union than our Canadian and British friends. Here we have a system of justice that's better than Canada or England. Ours is based on laws. Rules and regulations that must be followed. We call it a system of justice because judges are tasked with trying their best to make things right. A tall task for sure. I've tried my best over the years to give everyone who comes into my courtroom a fair hearing."

Now it seemed like the judge was playing for the cameras.

"What is the definition of justice?" he asked. He paused to let the room consider the question.

"Justice is the quality of being fair and reasonable. Mr. Martin purchased a lottery ticket. That fact is not in dispute. He chose the winning numbers. I'm convinced of that. Despite Mr. Dunn's dance around the issue, I think I'm safe in saying that the Lottery Commission agrees with the plaintiff that Mr. Martin did indeed purchase the winning ticket."

Are we going to win?

"The ticket was destroyed. Defendants argue it was a result of Plaintiff's negligence. Are they right? I suppose. Mrs. Martin, I've left things in my pockets as well. My wife has run them through the washing machine, and a few things have been destroyed. She wasn't very happy about it either."

He smiled at Eve when he said it.

"Don't blame yourself. These things happen."

Thank you for being kind to my wife but make your ruling!

"What if it hadn't been the plaintiff's fault? I said earlier that I don't deal with hypotheticals, but let's go down that rabbit hole for a moment. What if the Martins' house caught on fire and burned to the ground, destroying the ticket? What if a robber broke into their house and stole it? Would Mr. Martin be entitled to the prize even though he didn't follow the rules on the back of the ticket?"

I think so.

"What if he had a car accident on the way to the lottery office and the ticket was destroyed? What if he couldn't bring the intact ticket to the lottery office for whatever reason? Couldn't sign the back through no fault of his own? It's not always possible to follow the letter of the law. I've learned that over the years. I think we can all agree that it wouldn't be fair and reasonable under any of those circumstances. None of us would say, 'tough luck.' It wouldn't be justice. I could see myself ruling in Mr. Martin's favor under those circumstances. Perhaps the Lottery Commission would be sympathetic to his cause as well."

I like this judge.

"But alas, those aren't the circumstances. Hypotheticals are irrelevant to the facts of this case."

He said it almost with resignation.

We're going to lose.

"A judge must rule on the facts in front of him. While none of those hypotheticals are true, there are some facts that ground my decision. Given the fact that Mrs. Martin brought the remains of the ticket to court, and given the fact that we are dealing with a mutilated ticket and not a lost ticket, given the fact that the Powerball number is present on the fragment providing further evidence that the ticket that went through the wash is the winning ticket, given the fact that the Lottery Commission has paid prizes for damaged tickets in the past, it is my ruling that the only fair and reasonable thing to do is to award the prize to Mr. Martin and declare him the winner of the Powerball drawing!"

A collective gasp went through the crowd.

Did we win?

"That, in my mind, is justice. I rule in favor of the plaintiff and find that Mr. Martin is entitled to judgment as a matter of law. The court finds that he does have the winning ticket, and I am ordering the Lottery Commission to pay him the prize in its totality based on the procedures set in place for all lottery winners."

The crowd erupted in applause.

"Thank you, Your Honor," Rich heard Eve say over the din.

The judge gaveled the hearing over. He abruptly stood and walked out. Before the bailiff could even tell them to rise.

Leaving Rich stunned.

So much so that he couldn't move. He wasn't sure if he even took a breath until after the judge had left the courtroom.

Paul Jackson shook him back to reality. He slapped him on the back and hugged him profusely.

"We won! You did it! You get the money!"

Eve shrieked and bolted over the banister practically tackling him. She threw her arms around his neck and kissed him profusely all over his face.

Howard Dunn came over to congratulate them. The reporters crowded around. Frantically snapping pictures. Dunn reached out his hand.

Jackson shook it. Eve didn't let go of Rich. She kept clutching him.

"Congratulations," Dunn said.

"Are you going to appeal?" Jackson asked.

"I'll talk to my clients, but I don't think so. If the judge is satisfied that Mr. Martin deserves the money, then I suspect the Lottery Commission will agree."

He turned and walked out of the courtroom. None of the press followed him. They were interested in what Rich and Eve had to say. More had flooded in from the outside and had crowded around them. The sound of cameras clicking was almost deafening.

"How does it feel to win the largest lottery jackpot in history?" someone asked.

Rich answered. "It feels like a million bucks."

"A billion bucks," Eve said, with a girlish giggle.

The reporters bombarded them with questions. Eventually, Jackson put a stop to it and led them out of the courthouse and to his car.

Finally away from the mob, Eve collapsed in Rich's arms and sobbed. The weight of the last few days hit them both all at once.

He cried as well.

Tears of joy. The pressure was off of him. He could hardly believe it.

"I love you so much," Rich said, letting Eve's tears soak his shirt.

"I love you so much," she said.

"You did it," Rich said. "We won because of you. You found that ticket fragment."

"I'm so glad I'm married to you."

"Me too."

They kissed passionately. Ignoring the cameras snapping pictures through the window of the car.

"I want to remember this moment forever," Eve said, staring deep into his eyes.

"We have the rest of our lives together to remember it."

9

Seven years later

The law offices of Bailey and Banks smelled of old money being sustained by new. Rich and Eve had certainly made their contribution to the cause. Combined, they'd spent more than $250,000 on their divorce.

It had been more than six months since Eve filed for a dissolution of marriage and hired Pamela Banks from Bailey and Banks to represent her. Rich hired his own attorney who said an uncontested divorce could be obtained within thirty-one days in the state of Georgia. Contested divorces could drag on from six months to several years. Depending on how many big things had to be resolved.

While it didn't take several years to get to this point, Rich couldn't imagine a more contested divorce than theirs. Emotions got out of control right away and the couple found themselves fighting over almost everything. Big and small.

Actually, the bigger issues were the easiest to resolve. Eve would get the main house appraised at $13.3 million. Rich was fine with that. He didn't want to uproot their two kids from their home.

After they won the lottery, they decided to stay in Peach Ridge and build a house just outside the city limits. The couple had the money to build a mega church building on the same hundred acres as the house.

While Peach Ridge's population was under 3,000, more than 200,000 people lived within thirty minutes of the strategically placed building. With unlimited money to advertise, the church filled up almost immediately. The area was infatuated with Rich and Eve's story, and the so-called paparazzi gave them as much free advertising as what they paid for.

For more than a year, the press camped on their doorstep and was at every service. Recording their entire lives. They finally lost interest but resurfaced with the fervor of a crazed wildcat after word got around that Eve had filed for divorce.

The whole sordid affair had been devastating to Rich. Not only had he lost his marriage, but he lost the church. The happiest years of his life were watching the church grow from nothing to thousands. Before the proverbial fan hit, the church ran more than 7,000 people on Sunday mornings, making it one of the biggest churches in Georgia.

Rich was able to hire all the staff he wanted. The first thing he did was hire the best musicians he could find. With the state-of-the-art sound and audio-visual systems, they could put on quite a show.

The services were televised across the entire state. At some point, Rich intended to turn everything into a worldwide ministry.

Rich was in his element when he preached. He'd found his calling. He was a natural speaker, and in that setting what he lacked in experience he made up for with charisma and enthusiasm. The people responded and loved his messages.

And he had enough money available to cover up his mistakes. Which were many.

So much for best-laid plans.

Eve had been his biggest fan and loudest cheerleader. How ironic that she would be the impetus to getting him fired from a church for the second time in his brief preaching career by filing for divorce.

His heart ached thinking about it. He'd dreaded this day. Going to the office of her attorney to sign the final paperwork. This was it. In a few minutes, his marriage would be over.

He'd leave there with a huge sum of money but a heavy heart with no idea what he would do next.

Technically, the church didn't fire him. They didn't have that power. Rich owned the $28.5 million dollar building. He leased it back to the church for a dollar a year. Rich didn't take a salary. The church had a board of elders, but the bylaws didn't provide a way for them to terminate him. He could stay as long as he wanted.

When the scandal hit, he had no choice. The board threatened to resign. Half the people would leave. His reputation was already ruined.

Deciding who would end up with the church building in the divorce settlement wasn't difficult either. Eve wanted no part of it. Rich was somewhat surprised she even wanted to stay in the house, given its proximity to the church.

But she did, and he gladly gave it to her. She had done most of the work designing it anyway. He was busy running the church. She'd likely never step foot in that building again. He wasn't sure what he was going to do, since he was the landlord. He'd likely never go back there on a Sunday either.

Seeing another man in the pulpit would be as hard as seeing another man in Eve's bed.

Rich let out an internal groan just thinking about it. He sat next to Jason Leggett, his attorney. Eve and her attorney, Pamela Banks, sat across from them. The two attorneys were reviewing the final paperwork to make sure everything was in order.

Eve seemed just as nervous. She fidgeted with her hands when she was anxious and was rubbing them raw. Her eyes were fixed down on the table. They'd been in that room for more than ten minutes, and she had yet to look at Rich.

Jason got Rich's attention and pointed something out to him. He got the beach house in Myrtle Beach. Appraised at $4.3 million.

The beach house had been a much bigger issue than the main residence. Eve loved that home. They picked it out together a few months after they won the lottery. Paid cash for it. Made love half the night on the private beach the first day they got the keys.

She had insisted that she get the house.

"That's not fair!" he had said. "You can't get both houses."

"The kids love that house."

"They'll still get to go there with me."

"That's not the same."

"Then you shouldn't have divorced me."

"You shouldn't have cheated on me with the nanny."

"I didn't."

Rich didn't actually cheat on her with the nanny; it just looked like it.

The attorneys were finished.

"Everything is in order," Paul Leggett said.

"I'll read through the main points," Pamela Banks said. "So, the two parties are clear on the terms of the divorce agreement."

Divorce agreement! Ugh!

Rich could hardly believe he was hearing those words.

He suddenly felt numb. All emotion left him as Pamela Banks read from the agreement. Even his disdain for the bulldog of an attorney left him all at once. Like he was dead inside. The marriage was dead. The four people in the room were attending the funeral. Reading the divorce decree felt like someone reading the obituary.

The worst part of it was that all hope had left him as well. Up to that moment, he had held out hope that they'd never get to this point. He had suggested counseling. Eve refused. He had made all kinds of overtures, which she rejected.

Her heart was as cold as the inside of a prison cell.

He kept quoting the verse, *With God all things are possible.* Maybe that wasn't true. It didn't seem like even God could restore their marriage.

Eve's attorney had the final document in her hands and read a bunch of legalese. The first part he understood was when she said, "the reason for the divorce is irreconcilable differences."

The small victory he had managed to obtain in the war.

Georgia was not a no-fault divorce state. A reason had to be listed on the divorce decree. Eve had insisted that adultery be listed as the cause of the divorce. Rich had fought it vehemently. Spent thousands in attorney's fees arguing the point.

"I don't want the kids reading that someday," he had said.

"When they get older, they're going to find out," she retorted.

"I'll be able to give my side of the story."

"I'm not going to lie for you."

"I'm not asking you to."

"Just admit it. That's the real reason for the divorce."

"I'm not agreeing to it. I don't care."

Rich's attorney warned him that if they couldn't come to an agreement, then the judge would make the final decision. That would mean bringing up the entire sordid affair and airing all their dirty laundry in the courtroom.

"I might be able to keep the press out, and we can have the terms of the divorce agreement sealed, but it's going to leak out. The press will find out the details. Better to settle it outside of court."

"How do I come to an agreement with someone who is so unreasonable?" Rich had asked.

"Give her more money," his attorney said.

They fought over the issue for months, and the attorney bills were extravagant. Eventually Eve relented, and they agreed to irreconcilable differences for a sum that turned out to be a little over seventy-three million dollars.

Which still made Rich mad.

Pamela Banks drew his mind back to the task at hand.

"Ms. Martin will retain the primary residence."

It seemed strange to call her Ms. rather than Mrs. Eve had been so excited to be called Mrs. Rich Martin. At least she was keeping his last name but only because she wanted the same last name as the children.

"Mr. Martin we will retain the beach house in Myrtle Beach."

Rich thought he heard a moan of disgust from Eve.

The anger returned with a vengeance.

Did she think she was entitled to everything?

The hits kept on coming.

"The couple have liquid assets of $473,563,423.76. Mr. Martin will receive two hundred million of that amount, and Ms. Martin will be entitled to the balance.

Pamela Banks took out a cashier's check and handed it to Paul Leggett for his inspection. He looked it over and nodded his satisfaction. Then sat it on the conference table in front of him next to his file.

"As to personal effects, it's my understanding that the parties have agreed and are satisfied with the separation of assets. I'm told that Mr. Martin has already removed everything from the house that belonged to him."

Rich nodded. One of the worst days of his life. Moving all his clothes and items out of the house. He left everything else. All the furniture and such. Technically, he was entitled to half of everything, but wanted things to be as normal as possible for the kids. Not that he had a place to put furniture anyway.

For now, he was going to move into the beach house and then decide what to do later. At least he had two hundred million dollars to help soften the blow.

"Mr. Martin will receive the five sports cars and Ms. Martin will retain the SUV."

Rich chuckled to himself. He had five cars worth several hundred thousand dollars but no garage to house them in.

"I think that's everything related to the personal effects," Banks said.

"There's the matter of the golf clubs," Leggett said.

"Oh right."

Banks looked through her files.

"Ms. Martin intends to write Mr. Martin a check for $3,475.93. That was the amount agreed upon."

"I don't have my checkbook with me," Eve said sheepishly. Speaking for the first time.

"That shouldn't keep us from signing the agreement today," Banks said.

"We will have to hold the agreement until she can provide the check."

"I'll have a courier bring it to you later today."

"It's not necessary," Rich said. "I trust Eve. She can give it to me the next time I see her."

At that point, he didn't want anything to hold things up. All he wanted to do was get out of that office as soon as possible.

He wished he hadn't made the golf clubs such an issue. When he went to pick up his things they were missing.

"Where are my golf clubs?" he asked.

"I sold them," she said.

"Sold them!"

"At a pawn shop."

"For how much."

"A hundred bucks. I wanted them out of the garage. They were in the way of my car."

"You wanted to hurt me. You always complained about me spending too much time playing golf."

They'd gotten into a huge argument. The dispute was later taken up by the attorneys. Rich figured it cost somewhere around ten grand to resolve the issue.

So stupid.

"Let's move on to discuss custody of the children," Banks said. "The couple will maintain joint custody, and both parties agree to use their best faith efforts to keep the children's interest above their own."

"That's what I intend to do," Rich said.

"Neither party is allowed to say anything disparaging about the other in front of the children," Banks said.

"Understood."

Eve nodded, but still didn't look at Rich.

"Mr. Martin will have the children two weekends a month and four weeknights a month. Holidays will be alternated. The parties agree to give the other twenty-four-hour notice if they are not going to pick up the children at the designated times."

She paused to see if there was any objection.

We'd gone over all this ad nauseam.

"Mr. Martin agrees to pay child support in the amount of sixty-thousand dollars a month.

Rich didn't think he should have to pay that.

"I gave you seventy-three million dollars," he had argued. "That should be more than enough."

"The law mandates child support," Leggett had explained. If Rich didn't agree to an amount, the judge would decide, and Rich wouldn't want that. He might make it twice that amount and order alimony on top of it.

So, he had agreed.

Divorce was expensive. It'd be easier in some ways if they hadn't won the lottery. They'd probably still be together and madly in love.

"There's one final issue my client would like to bring up," Pamela Banks said.

Rich groaned.

Eve glared at him. The first time she had looked him in the eye.

"My client would like for Mr. Martin to agree that he will not introduce their children to any woman who is not his fiancé or wife. No girlfriends."

"I don't have a girlfriend," Rich said.

"Yeah, right," Eve said.

Paul Leggett spoke up. "Mr. Martin is a single man as of a few minutes from now. As such, he is entitled to have any relationship that he wants and is allowed to introduce children to that person if he so desires."

Banks started to say something, but Leggett cut her off.

"With all due respect, Pamela, you know that the judge would never order that. He'd throw us out of court if we brought this issue before him with all the other issues resolved."

Banks leaned over and whispered something in Eve's ear.

"I'll agree to it," Rich said bitterly, "if she'll agree to the same thing. She won't introduce the kids to any of her boyfriends."

"That won't be an issue with me," she said. "I don't intend to even date anyone anytime soon."

"Me neither."

"Yeah. Right."

"Should we put this in writing?" Banks said.

"Is that really necessary?" Leggett asked. "We're all adults here. The couple has agreed to the point, and both parties are counting on the other to keep their ends of this agreement."

"Fine by me," Rich said.

"Me, too," Eve snorted.

"Okay then," Banks said.

She took her copy and set it in front of Eve and gave her a pen to sign it.

Leggett had already shoved his copy in front of Rich who signed it roughly.

They exchanged documents, and Eve signed the document Rich signed, and he signed hers. Leggett gave the document back to Banks who said, "I'll have these notarized and sent over to the court immediately."

"When will the divorce be final?" Eve asked.

"Sounds like it won't be soon enough for you," Rich said.

Leggett touched Rich's arm. A gesture telling him to be quiet. They were about done.

"I will file the document with the court this afternoon," Banks said. "As soon as the judge signs the order, then the divorce will be final. Next day or two. Regardless, you can consider yourselves divorced."

"Then that should do it," Leggett said. He stood to his feet and extended his hand to Banks who shook it.

Rich stood. Eve remained seated. He looked in her eyes to see if there were any tears. Nothing.

"I'm sorry," Rich said. The words came out of his mouth like an unexpected cough.

Eve bit her lip and nodded. The only eye contact was out of the corner of her eye.

Before anyone could move toward the door, they heard a loud noise coming from the main office area outside the conference room.

Gunshots.

Then screaming.

Shouting.

More shots fired.

The conference room was surrounded by windows on both sides. One side looked out onto the street below. The other side gave a clear view of the main reception area.

Rich saw the image of a man carrying a machine gun wearing a bullet-proof vest.

He was shouting. People were on the ground. Some were cowering behind desks.

Rich could barely make out what he was saying, but it was unmistakable.

"Where is she?" he demanded. "Where is Pamela Banks?"

Someone pointed toward the conference room. He looked that way. Banks had ducked down under the conference table. As had Eve.

The gunman walked toward them with his gun raised and pointed directly at them.

Before Rich or Leggett could react, he was there. In the room.

His eyes blazed in rage.

10

The gunman had a crazed look on his face. The most concerning thing was that he had his finger on the trigger of an assault rifle. Rich didn't know the brand of the weapon but figured that the magazine held at least thirty bullets. Probably more.

The man was outfitted for war. He had on a belt with more magazines, a knife, and a small handgun. His face wasn't concealed, meaning he didn't care if the authorities knew who he was. Probably figuring he wasn't getting out of there alive. Which meant the odds were great that they might not either.

It didn't take long to figure out that the gunman knew Pamela Banks, and his vendetta was with her.

"Banks, get out from under the table!" he barked. "Now!"

She slowly rose to her feet with her hands raised in surrender. Her eyes widened in terror.

Eve remained on the floor, hidden under the table. It wasn't clear if the gunman knew she was there. Rich and his attorney were on the side of the table nearest the door. The man was just inside the door and not more than five feet away from Rich.

"Mr. Curry, let's talk about this," Banks said, her voice cracking. Rich could see her body tremble.

"The time for talking is over," Curry said. "Get up against the wall. Over there."

He waved the gun toward the far corner of the room.

"Who's that on the floor? Stand up!" he demanded.

Rich's heart sank. The gunman did know that Eve had hidden under the table.

She rose slowly to her feet. Took one look at the gunman, then at Rich, then back at the gunman. Her face was white as a brand-new bed sheet.

The gunman looked at Rich.

"Is that your wife?"

"Ex-wife," Rich said.

Curry laughed.

"And Banks is representing her?"

"Yes."

"Did she take you to the cleaners like she did me?"

"Pretty much."

"That's what she does. She's evil, man. She'll rip your heart right out of your chest."

It did sort of feel like that. Before, Rich felt numb. Now all the emotions came flooding back like a tsunami. Destroying everything in its path. He could feel the gunman's rage and was channeling it himself.

He could only imagine what Banks and his ex-wife had done to this man to bring him to this point. Did he intend to kill her? Them?

"Get over there by your attorney," Curry said to Eve.

She immediately complied with his order. Banks reached out and pulled Eve close. They clutched hands and looked at the gunman for more instructions.

"Who are you?" Curry asked Leggett.

"I represent Mr. Martin in the divorce."

"You can go," the gunman said out of the blue. "You're one of the good guys."

Leggett didn't wait for the man to change his mind. He went straight for the door and was through it in a flash. Not even bothering to take his files with him.

"You too," he said to Rich. "I ain't got no beef with you."

Rich shook his head.

"I'm not leaving. Not without my wife."

The gunman twisted his lips to his side in confusion. "I thought you said she was your ex-wife."

"That's what I meant."

Rich still felt the rage, but his love for Eve had overpowered it and was at the forefront of his emotions. He felt an overwhelming urge to protect her. Which was foolish. Nothing he could do against all that firepower. Even if the gunman didn't have those weapons, he was a massive man. With huge biceps and forearms. His neck was seemingly the size of a tree trunk.

Rich was small in stature. He'd never been in a fight. A girl half the gunman's size could probably overpower Rich if she wanted to.

"If you know what's good for you, you'll leave," the gunman said.

Rich shook his head.

"I can't leave without her."

The gunman laughed again. Which seemed out of place considering the circumstance.

"I get it. You still love her." He looked over at Eve who was now huddled in the corner with her attorney. "I can see why. She's a pretty one."

"I suppose I do."

"Me, too. I still love my wife. They make you fall in love with them, then they stomp on your heart like an elephant." His words dripped with bitterness.

"I know how you feel," Rich said. "But killing her attorney isn't going to solve anything."

"No. But I can keep her from doing to others what she did to you and me. She ain't defending any more women if she's dead."

If Rich didn't figure out a way to diffuse the situation, this wasn't going to end well.

"Now get out of here," the gunman said roughly. "Before I change my mind."

"I can't. Not without Eve."

"You're a fool. You're going to get yourself killed."

"Maybe."

The gunman looked at his wrist to see the time. Rich could hear the sirens outside. The gunman obviously heard them too. Something would have to happen soon. Rich could imagine the police bursting through the doors of the office at any time.

"Make yourself useful, then," the gunman said. "Lock that door."

He pointed to the door of the conference room. He kept the gun on Rich as he walked over to the door and locked it.

"Lower all the blinds to the windows," he said next.

The conference room door and windows had blinds. Rich lowered them.

"Now the windows to the outside. Pull down the blinds."

Rich did as he was told. Good thing the blinds were easy to maneuver because Rich's hands shook like branches in the breeze.

The gunman put his gun over his shoulder.

"Help me with this table."

Rich knew what he meant. He wanted to barricade them in. The gunman moved the chairs to the side, then stepped to one end of the table. Rich went to the other. Together they pushed the massive table to its side and up against the door and windows.

Although the gunman did most of the heavy lifting. Rich struggled to get his side up against the windows but managed.

"Now, get over in that other corner," the gunman said to Rich. He pointed to the opposite corner from where Eve and Banks were standing.

While Rich did as he was told, the gunman walked toward Banks. Eve let out a muted scream. The gunman ordered Banks to put her hands out. She did while pleading for him not to harm her. He bound her wrists with zip ties. Then practically threw her to the ground.

"Get over there by your husband," the gunman said to Eve.

Eve walked quickly to his side of the room. Rich held out his arm. She shunned him at first, then accepted the embrace.

"Look at them," Curry said to Banks, mockingly. "I bet they were madly in love at one time. Now she will barely even let him touch her. That's what you do to people. Destroy their love."

"It's already destroyed by the time they get to me," Banks retorted. "I didn't cause it. All I do is protect my client's interests. I can't help it if I'm good at it."

The gunman exploded in a flurry of harsh words. Calling her every name he could get out of his mouth at one time. For a moment, Rich thought he was going to shoot her on the spot. Banks put her hands in front of her face to defend herself.

For whatever reason, he stepped away.

The gunman looked over at Rich and Eve.

"She made me out to be the bad guy," he said angrily. "I'm not the bad guy."

Rich could think of several reasons why that wasn't true but kept his mouth shut.

"My wife cheated on me," the gunman said. "Can you imagine that? And she's the one who got the kids. That woman over there made it look like the whole divorce was my fault."

Curry was pacing now. With purpose in his steps.

"Did your wife cheat on you?" he asked Rich.

Rich looked at Eve. He felt the pained expression on his face when his eyes met hers. He could see the fear in her eyes but also her accusations. If only he knew how to take it away. Convince her what she believed wasn't true.

Tears began to trickle down Eve's face.

"He cheated on me," she said, sending another dagger through Rich's already damaged heart.

"Then you got what you deserved," the gunman said to Rich. "Why would any man cheat on a woman that beautiful?"

"I didn't."

"Yeah. That's what my wife said, even though I caught her in the act. She tried to make me think I was wrong. I know what I saw."

Rich still had his arm around Eve. She was shivering like the temperature was below freezing. Rich was sweating.

"Both of you, get down on the floor," the gunman said.

He continued to pace. Mumbled to himself. It appeared that he had gotten more agitated talking about his wife.

A few minutes later, the phone pierced the silence, since no one had said anything for a good five minutes.

"Do you want me to answer it?" Rich asked.

"No. I ain't ready to talk to no one yet."

The gunman was a typical Georgian with a deep southern drawl. What was usually described as a good-ole-boy accent. His voice didn't always match his appearance. Half the time, he was soft spoken. Even when he was angry and raised his voice, it lacked authenticity. Rich believed the man really was a good man. He'd just gone off the deep end. Driven by the circumstances and a broken heart.

That didn't justify the behavior, it only helped Rich to understand it. The pastor in him came out. The man he had been for the last seven years. He had his faults, but he genuinely loved preaching and helping people. Something he already desperately missed.

"Because of her," he pointed his gun at Banks, "I had to pay my wife child support. Can you believe it? Banks told the judge I was unstable. Can you imagine that?"

Rich actually could. Considering the man's current behavior.

"I gotta pay her fourteen-hundred dollars a month. I only make twenty-eight bucks an hour. I take home about fifteen hundred every two weeks. Dang government of ours, those crooks, take almost half of it. How am I supposed to live on the rest? I had to move out of our house and get an apartment. It's a dump. She gets to live in our house with her boyfriend."

"That's rough," Rich said. "I understand how you feel."

Sort of. Rich would be moving into a four-million-dollar beach house. He imagined the loneliness would feel the same though.

Eve had pulled away from him and although they sat in the corner together, inches apart, it seemed like miles. She was cold and distant again.

"How much did she take you for a month?" the gunman asked.

Rich laughed. "You wouldn't believe it if I told you."

"How much? A couple of grand?"

"Sixty-thousand dollars a month."

His mouth flew open. "You lie!"

"I swear. That's the truth."

His eyes widened. "I know you," he said excitedly. "You're that couple that won the lottery. Over a billion dollars. You lucky son of a gun."

Rich didn't feel so lucky at the moment. At least a dozen times over the last few months, he wished they'd never won that money.

"That's us."

"Your wife washed the ticket."

"That was my fault," Rich said. "I left the ticket in my shirt pocket."

"Everything is our fault when it comes to women."

"This time, it really was my fault."

"I thought you looked familiar, but I couldn't place it."

The phone rang again. Curry angrily unplugged it from the wall. Fortunately, he didn't rip it out, so it still worked. Perhaps he wanted to keep his options open. Which might be a good sign.

"I ain't talking to nobody," he said.

"What happens next?" Rich dared to ask.

"I haven't decided."

"Maybe talking to the authorities would be a good idea. You could work out some kind of deal. Heck, I'd even testify for you. You seem like a decent guy who got the bad end of the stick."

His tone turned sober. "I got nothing to say to them. I came here to kill Banks and then myself. And that's what I'm going to do. I just haven't decided when to do it."

"You don't have to do that," Rich said. Keeping his voice calm even though his heart was beating out of his chest.

"Ah ... That's right. You're some kind of pastor."

"Yeah. I was, anyway."

"I don't want to hear all your religious talk. I've heard it all before. Save it. Grew up in a church. I was baptized when I was nine. I know the Bible as well as you."

"That's probably true."

"How did you end up here?" Curry said. "Why did you cheat?"

Rich could tell the gunman was softening a bit and tiring. The adrenaline was probably crashing inside of him. From Rich's vantage point he could see the shadows on the other side of the conference room windows. Law enforcement had obviously taken up positions in the lobby.

Curry noticed as well and sat with his back against the conference table. Rich couldn't see a scenario where the law enforcement could get inside of the room and disarm the gunman before he killed Banks and himself. Maybe even them if he wanted.

Rich didn't want to answer the question. He didn't know how to respond without making Eve even angrier. He'd argued his denials until he was blue in the face. She simply didn't believe him and never would.

"He cheated on me with our nanny," Eve said bitterly. Speaking for the first time since the man entered the room.

"I did not!" Rich exclaimed.

"I saw you kissing her."

"You saw her kissing me."

The exchange got heated. They'd had this same argument a dozen times before. Maybe more.

Rich turned to Curry and explained.

"The nanny hit on me from the moment we hired her. I walked her to the door one night, when she planted one on my lips. Right out of the blue. I was shocked."

"It sure looked to me like you were enjoying it," Eve said with sarcasm dripping from the words.

When it happened, Rich was in such shock that he didn't pull away immediately. He should have, but it had been several years since Eve had kissed him with that passion, and he didn't know how to respond. Or he knew but was weak.

"She walked in right when it happened," Rich said defensively. "Do you think I would be stupid enough to kiss our nanny at the front door with my wife and kids in the other room?"

"I walked in on my wife with another man in my own house," Curry said. "She lied and said nothing happened. But I saw the bed messed up. She tried to make me think I was crazy. So yes. It does happen."

"Well, it didn't happen with me. I wasn't interested in her at all. I think she wanted something to happen so she could try to extort money out of us."

"Which she did!" Eve said. "You paid her $75,000. Why would you pay her money if nothing happened?"

"You know why. To make it go away."

"Tell him about the other three ladies you had to make go away."

"You cheated four times?" Curry said. "Boy, you get around."

The only good thing about the conversation was the gunman had removed his finger off the trigger. Clearly amused by the story and watching Rich squirm.

Eve was as loaded with accusations as the assault rifle was with bullets.

"I didn't cheat with any of those four women," Rich said defensively. "They were all trying to get money from me because I was rich. No pun intended."

Curry laughed, which seemed to ease the tension in the room even more. They might actually get out of this alive if he could earn Curry's trust.

Eve was another matter. He'd never be able to earn back her trust.

"I didn't know about the three other women," Eve said, angrily, speaking directly to the gunman. It's as if he was a marriage counselor and the two of them were trying to convince him to take their side. "I had to find out about it at a meeting of the elders of our church. Do you know how embarrassing that was?"

"That was unfortunate," Rich said.

After Rich refused to pay the nanny, she contacted the elders, and they called a meeting. The board insisted that Eve attend. That's when it was decided to pay the nanny $75,000. As the meeting was about to adjourn, someone mentioned the other three ladies who had also threatened to sue Rich.

The board had settled with each one of them for $10,000. Under the table. No one else knew about it.

Rich had brought each situation to the board for that very reason. To give himself cover in case it came out. He knew the board would believe him over the women. Which they did. The church was doing so well, the last thing it needed was a sex scandal. Especially one founded on false allegations.

It seemed like the right thing to do at the time.

When it came up, Eve pretended to know about the other three women in front of the board. When they got home, she was furious.

"I'm a target," Rich had argued. "These girls know we have a lot of money. It's not my fault."

"Maybe it *is* your fault. Maybe you led them on. Like you did the nanny."

Rich had to admit that he was friendly with them. He didn't intend anything by it. That didn't mean he had cheated though.

Things were never the same after that. Eve didn't believe he wasn't carrying on with the nanny and filed for divorce shortly thereafter. No amount of explaining would change her mind.

Rich eventually accepted his fate because he was riddled with guilt. He somehow felt like the whole thing was his fault. After Eve gave birth to their second child, they had grown apart. The money had changed them. They weren't close anymore or communicating. Rich poured into his church work, and Eve focused on the kids and her friends.

Sex was rare and Rich was lonely for attention from a woman.

When Eve eventually filed for divorce, he didn't put up much of a fight. He felt like he deserved what he got. What he hadn't expected was the backlash at church. The board forced him to resign and grovel before the church and admit his sins. Rich denied any wrongdoing with the four women but had to reveal to the congregation that Eve had filed for divorce and the church had paid out money for the settlements. Even though Rich paid the money himself, it still made him look guilty.

And here they were, where they never thought he'd be. Divorced from his wife. The signed divorce papers lay on the floor next to the conference table. His two-hundred-million-dollar check was somewhere in the heap as well.

Curry was nervous again. Fidgeting. Playing with the trigger. At times the gun was pointed at Rich and Eve. Not necessarily on purpose. Carelessness on Curry's part.

Rich couldn't help but wonder if he'd ever get a chance to spend those two-hundred-million dollars.

11

Regina Burrows sat in a dentist chair getting a root canal when her phone buzzed with an alert. The right side of her face was numb, and the dentist seemed annoyed, but she had to answer it. The sound of the tone meant the call was from the Sheriff's office.

"Burrows," she answered. Which sounded something like "her brows" given her inability to articulate words given the condition of her mouth.

"We've got a hostage situation at a law office," the dispatcher on the line said. "They need you there immediately."

"Can you send Reilly?" Regina mumbled, already knowing the answer.

"He's on a domestic."

If he weren't on another call, they would've called him first. She was backup.

They dealt with an average of four crisis situations a month. Most of them domestic disputes. Those were usually resolved quickly, but some could go on for hours. No telling how long Reilly would be tied up.

A hostage taker wouldn't wait for them to work out their schedules.

Regina had trained Reilly herself and was confident in his abilities. He'd resolve the situation on his own timetable based on the circumstances at the scene.

Truth be told, she needed two more Reillys. Two teams would be ideal. Budget cuts didn't allow it, and they simply didn't have enough hostage situations. So, when one of them went on vacation or took a day off, this scenario was always in the back of her mind.

So far, nothing had come up at the same time, and they'd been effective in their work. Since Regina was put in charge of the hostage-negotiation team eight years ago, they'd only had one death. A record she was proud of.

When the dentist called that morning and said he had an unexpected opening, she jumped on it. The tooth had ached for more than three weeks, and her appointment to get it fixed wasn't scheduled for another two weeks.

What were the odds of two hostage situations occurring at the same time? Obviously, better than she had calculated.

"What's the sit ... ua ... tion?" she said slowly, so the person on the other end could understand her. At the same time reminding herself to choose shorter words.

"Ex husband. One of the attorneys in the firm represented his wife."

"What's the firm?"

"Bailey and Banks."

Regina was familiar with it.

"Weapon?"

"Assault rifle and handgun."

"No bomb?"

"The one witness didn't see anything."

"Witness?"

"The gunman released one of the hostages immediately."

She wondered why but didn't ask. The fewer words the better. But she also only wanted the most important information first. How many people were still being held hostage was more important than how many had been released.

"Do we know the gunman's name?"

"Wes Curry."

"Where's he holed up?"

"Barricaded in a conference room."

"Any contact?"

"We tried, but he unplugged the phone in the office. His cell phone is off."

"How many hostages?"

"Three."

"Any angles?" Meaning any line of sight to the gunman. Sometimes a sniper could get a shot off from an adjacent building, if necessary.

"The room has a whole wall of windows to the outside, but blinds prevent a shot. We're inside the premises near the room. We've got a SWAT team on the scene ready to go in. They're waiting for someone to tell them what to do."

"Tell them not to go in unless they absolutely have no choice. I'll get there as soon as I can."

"Got it."

She hung up the phone. The dentist still hovered over her. He had at least moved the light, so it didn't shine in her eyes.

"I have to go," Regina said.

"I'm not finished with the root canal," the dentist said.

"It's an emergency."

He shook his head.

"You can't go out like that. That tooth is open. If you leave now, you may find yourself in your own emergency. I must at least close it and put a temporary filling in."

"How long will that take?"

"I'll be as quick as I can. Twenty minutes, tops."

She leaned back in the chair.

"Do it in ten."

* * *

Rich and Eve had been arguing for more than ten minutes. Rich wanted to avoid a confrontation with her, but she provoked him when she said to the gunman, "There were actually five women."

The gunman seemed disinterested. He still sat on the floor with his back against the conference table. Obviously concerned about the force of people who had assembled outside the door. Every time he heard a sound coming from that direction, he strained to look.

The problem was the gun. Pointed right at Rich and Eve. The gunman's finger fidgeted on the trigger. Rich was concerned the gun could go off accidentally. Or on purpose if he got any more agitated with them.

"Why don't you two shut up?" the gunman finally said, when the argument between Rich and Eve became more heated. "I'm tired of hearing about all your problems. Both of you are ridiculous. You have millions of dollars, and you still can't make a relationship work."

"You shut up!" Eve said. "Our problems are none of your business. We listened to you complain about your wife for fifteen minutes."

The gunman had unloaded his burdens on them. Rich initiated that conversation. At first, he tried to keep the gunman preoccupied. To get his mind off shooting somebody. As time passed, he saw it as a ministry opportunity. The pastor in him genuinely cared about the man. Who was acting out of hurt.

In a weird way, Rich knew how he felt. He couldn't imagine how he'd feel if Eve had cheated on him.

He heard the Holy Spirit say to him in a still small voice, *Like Eve feels now.*

I didn't cheat on her.

She doesn't know that.

I told her.

Keep telling her. Try to understand why she's hurt.

Rich tried to imagine how he'd feel if he had walked in on Eve kissing another man. The thought made his heart ache. He'd be devastated. Probably imagine the worst at first. He felt sympathy for Eve and for the gunman.

Actually, the gunman had it worse. He walked in on his wife after having sex with another man. While it didn't justify wielding a gun and taking hostages, Rich could imagine how hopeless he must feel. Especially, since the divorce was final, and the man had moved into their house. Which his wife got in the settlement.

Thanks to Pamela Banks. The woman cowering in the corner like a scared puppy. Her hands bound. Her makeup smeared from tears.

The same woman who had cost Rich seventy-three million dollars even though she had to know how unfair her demands were. He could see how it might drive a man to act irrationally. While he never thought of killing Banks, he caught himself hating her on more than one occasion.

God had helped him forgive to an extent. Not fully. Forgiving Banks and Eve was a work in progress.

Which was why Rich wanted to help the man out of the predicament he had put himself in. Taking another life and going to jail for the rest of his life wouldn't solve anything. Or taking his own life.

Rich somehow had to convince him of that fact. If the man really was a Christian, then he needed to know that God would somehow work this together for his good if he would allow it.

A clock on the wall confirmed it had been two hours since the gunman burst into the room. Rich wondered why the authorities hadn't acted or at least tried to make contact with the gunman. It seemed like something should've happened by now.

In a way, Rich was glad the authorities were taking their time. For a few minutes, he thought he was making progress with the gunman. Having someone to talk to seemed to be unburdening him.

When Rich thought things were better, the gunman mentioned that he thought this wasn't the first time his wife had cheated on him, even though he didn't have proof. That's when Eve dropped the grenade in the middle of the room, setting off the argument.

"My husband cheated on me with five women," Eve said, matter-of-factly, like she had stated the sky was blue.

"What are you talking about?" Rich asked, trying to mute the anger that had suddenly exploded inside of him like an erupting volcano. Distracting him from his goal of diffusing the situation with the gunman.

"There's the woman at the first church," Eve said bitterly. "Peach Ridge Community. Rich was the pastor."

More often than not, Eve directed her words to the gunman. A passive aggressive approach meant to hurt him. It did. The entire day had been hard on his emotions, and Eve was purposefully trying to cause him more pain.

"What woman?" Rich asked.

"Don't tell me you've forgotten about her. She's why you got fired from the church."

"Are you talking about the lady whose car broke down? With the two girls? The same day we found out we won the lottery?"

"Yeah. That's her."

"You know nothing happened with her," he practically shouted. "She ran out of gas like I said. I stopped and helped her."

"That's your story and you're obviously sticking to it."

"Because that's what happened."

"I don't believe you."

"You said you did at the time."

"I did. That's before I knew what kind of man you are."

"What's that supposed to mean?"

"Do you really want me to answer that question?"

He really didn't.

Instead, he said, "I can't believe you're bringing her up. I don't even remember her name."

"Why would a pastor have a strange woman in his car?" Eve said, directing the question toward the gunman which infuriated Rich even more.

The gunman ignored Eve. He seemed preoccupied. He kept looking over his shoulder at the door.

Rich exploded. Unable to control himself.

"It was a hundred degrees outside!" he shouted. "I wasn't going to leave those two girls and that poor woman in the hot sun. It wasn't safe."

"Yeah right. I doubt there were even two girls. The person who saw her in the car with you didn't see any kids."

"They were sitting in the back," he said defensively. "They wouldn't be able to see them. That doesn't mean they weren't there."

"Whatever."

"Eve. That's what happened. I swear. The two gas containers were still in my car. Remember?" He asked the question mockingly.

"Whatever."

Rich hated it when she said that. She didn't used to. That became her go to word over the last couple of years when they argued.

That's when the gunman told them to shut up again.

"The two of you act like you're still married," he added.

"Technically, we are," Eve said. "Those are our divorce papers on the floor over there. The divorce is not final until the judge signs the orders. Which he can't do because some idiot is holding us hostage!"

"You got a real mouth on you," the gunman said, angrily.

In less than a minute, Eve had ruined all the progress Rich had made over the last hour. She sneered at the gunman by twisting her lips to the side and adding a glare. Something Rich had seen on more than one occasion.

"I don't know how you can stand her," the gunman said to Rich.

"Hey! You can't talk about my wife like that."

"Why are you defending her? After the way she talks about you."

"She's not that bad," Rich said. "She's just mad at me."

"If my wife talked to me like that, I would've cheated on her too."

That clearly made Eve angry.

"Are you saying it's my fault that my husband cheated on me?"

"I didn't cheat on you," Rich said. "I wish you'd quit saying that."

Eve ignored him and kept her focus on the gunman.

"Why did your wife cheat on you? Is it your fault?"

Rich could see the gunman seething. He wanted to remind Eve that the man had a gun. She seemed not to care.

"No, it's not my fault," the gunman said. "I was a good husband."

"Somehow, I doubt that," Eve retorted.

"For what it's worth," the gunman said, looking at Rich, "I believe you."

"Thank you," Rich said.

"Of course, you would take his side. You men stick together," Eve said.

"Although, I wouldn't blame you if you did cheat on her," the gunman mumbled.

"I'm sure you were a real hoot to be married to!" Eve said, her words dripped with sarcasm.

Her fists were balled, and her jaw clenched. Rich grabbed her hands and stared her down.

She made that same sneer directed at him as she pulled her hands away.

"I don't think you should provoke him," Rich said barely above a whisper.

Eve was feisty that way. The stubborn Eve had come out now that she had channeled her fear into anger. One of the things he loved about her was her spunkiness. But that character trait made him nervous now, given the situation.

Banks sat in the corner keeping her mouth shut. A good thing considering anything she said would only provoke the situation even more.

Eve did enough provoking for all of them.

She was relentless.

"When are you going to let us out of here?" Eve asked the gunman roughly. "I have to go to the bathroom."

"I don't know."

"You can't hold us here forever."

The gunman looked at Rich. "You can still go if you want. I would if I were you."

"Like I said, I'm not leaving without her."

"She ain't going nowhere."

"Then neither am I."

Eve leaned over and whispered to Rich.

"You should go."

"I'm not leaving without you."

"What about our kids? Think about them. What if we both die? At least one of us needs to live through this so they don't lose both parents."

Rich hadn't thought about that. Eve was right. He should go. The most prudent thing to do.

The thought of leaving Eve ripped through his heart like a tornado through a neighborhood. Leaving a path of destruction. Divorced and living without her would be hard enough. The thought of never seeing her again caused an excruciating pain and made him tear up.

How could he walk out of that room and leave her in the hands of a madman? *What if he never saw her again?* The pain caused by that thought was unbearable.

The gunman was right. He did still love her.

Before Rich could make a decision, the gunman abruptly said, "You're right, sister. I'm tired of hearing your voice. Let's put an end to this. One way or the other."

What did that mean?

12

Regina arrived at the law offices nearly two hours after the first 911 call. Not ideal. It couldn't be helped. The dentist took at least twenty minutes. Then she hit traffic, delaying her further.

Fortunately, things were status quo. Nothing had changed since the police arrived on the scene. Her first task was to assess the situation and get all the facts.

The main reception area had furniture turned over and papers strewn. The gunman had entered the lobby and riddled the sign above the reception desk with bullets. That told her he had a weapon with a magazine based on the number of holes made in that short of time.

She was briefed by the sheriff in charge of the scene until she arrived.

Most of the information he provided came from the attorney in the conference room when the incident occurred. The one hostage who had been released. Regina wouldn't waste time talking to Mr. Leggett. It seemed like he had been thoroughly interviewed.

According to the attorney, two of the hostages were Mr. Rich Martin and his wife Eve. The other hostage was Eve's attorney. They met that morning to sign their final divorce decree.

The sheriff mentioned that the couple were lottery winners, although Regina already knew that. She remembered the names. The pair were all over the news about seven years ago when they won the biggest jackpot in lottery history. While she didn't remember all the details, she seemed to remember the wife washed the ticket in the laundry. A judge gave them the money anyway.

The husband was the pastor of a large church right outside of Peach Ridge. *So sad.* Although not surprising. A lot of the incidents she dealt with in her job were rooted in money.

The lottery probably had a part in destroying this marriage. That's why she never played the lottery. A waste of money, but also winning would cause too many headaches to deal with.

When the couple first won all that money, Regina bet they never thought they'd be in this situation. Not just divorce court, but now their lives were in danger.

The mountain of responsibility came over her as it always did when she arrived at a scene. One wrong move and she could get them killed. Their fate might very well depend on how well she handled the gunman.

She looked around the room, completely dissatisfied. They had the resources they needed, but they were set up wrong. The sheriff had handed her a radio headset and microphone when she first arrived, so she could communicate with everyone.

The numbness had started to wear off in her mouth, but she still had trouble articulating her orders with the authority she usually mustered behind the words. Everyone in the room had headsets on the same frequency, so she could speak directly. The gunman wouldn't be able to hear them.

Seven members of the SWAT team were at her disposal and two sheriff's deputies.

"I want the two deputies behind the reception desk," she said. "With guns on the door."

The men were standing around. With their guns holstered. If the gunman were to open fire suddenly, they'd be sitting ducks. Likely unable to react fast enough. She needed to get them to a safer spot.

The SWAT team was assembled together in the corner of the room out of the line of fire. With more professionalism and obviously more experience. With shields to protect them in the event of an attack. Their weapons were pointed down but on ready.

"SWAT. I want three of you to take a position by the south corner of the conference room. One of you will need the battering ram. The other four back them up."

"Roger that."

The conference table inside the room blocked the door but wasn't long enough to cover the entire wall. If they needed to breach the room, that'd be the place to do it. The battering ram could break the window and the other two members could be through the broken pane within seconds.

From what she could tell, the gunman sat on the floor using the conference table as protection. One hostage was in the far right-hand corner. The other two were in the left-hand corner of the room. It's good that they were separated. A better scenario if a gunfight broke out.

"Does anyone know if the gunman is right or left-handed?" Regina asked.

"I'll check with Mr. Leggett," the sheriff replied.

"He's right-handed," he answered within a few seconds. "Or at least he held the gun with his right hand on the trigger."

Regina envisioned the room. If the gunman was behind the conference room with his back to the table, that meant the gun faced toward the left side of the room. Confirming she had made the right decision placing SWAT on the right corner. Unlikely the gunman could change positions fast enough to get a shot off before one member of the SWAT team could take him out.

"Turn off all the lights in this room," she ordered. "Leave the lights in the conference room on."

She didn't want the gunman to be able to see their movements or even their shadows.

Regina took up a position on the floor next to the two deputies, behind the reception desk. The massive L-shaped structure would provide protection from an onslaught of bullets, should they come.

She always assumed the worst-case scenario. The man inside was driven by passion. Which made him more unpredictable than someone driven by ideology or calculation. But not less dangerous. With him, she'd have to overcome his emotions, the feelings driving the rage. In other situations, she had to deal with a gunman logically. Appeal to his thoughts.

What she needed to do now was figure out how to get in contact with him. He had disconnected the phone in the conference room. The phone was monitored in case he plugged it back in. Attempts to reach the hostage cell phones had been unsuccessful as well. The gunman probably seized them, or they were off.

Regina took a deep breath even though her heart beat at a steady pace. She took several minutes to think. Trying to decide what to do next.

The only thing she could think of was to walk up to the door and invite herself in. Without her gun. She couldn't take it inside the room for obvious reasons. At least, encourage the man to plug the phone back in. So they could talk.

Regina didn't move right away, even though the decision was made. She had a process, a routine.

First rule of hostage negotiations. Slow everything down. If possible.

In this case, it might be. The gunman hadn't killed anyone even though he had plenty of opportunity to do so. He also hadn't made any demands. Meaning he wasn't sure what to do. Or if he knew what he wanted to do, something held him back.

Her job was to find out what that something was. First, she needed to run through her checklist to make sure she had everything covered.

Step one, make contact without getting shot. If she failed at step one, none of the others mattered.

Step two, find out what he wanted. Building rapport was key. She wouldn't become his best friend, but she was good at making connections. Regina was likable and had a trustworthy and convincing tone to her voice.

Step three, build rapport. Open-ended questions would do that. Minimal encouragement would reinforce it. She'd use words like, "I see. Okay. I understand. That makes sense."

Empathy was powerful when she could provide it with believability.

The ultimate goal was influence. To get him to do something she wanted him to do. Like release Mr. and Mrs. Martin. The innocent bystanders. Regina was encouraged by the information provided by Mr. Leggett. The gunman had told Mr. Martin he could leave but not his wife. That meant his beef was with the women in the room.

Maybe she'd start there. At least get Mr. Martin out of the room. He might not leave. He didn't the first time. Why not? Probably for his ex-wife's benefit. To show her he was still willing to protect her.

Not a smart move. The couple had two young kids. Mr. Martin should've left to ensure one of them got out of this alive. The husband worried her. He might take matters into his own hands and try to become a hero in front of his ex-wife. Maybe as a way to win her back. Leggett had said the wife was the one who filed for divorce.

The last thing she needed was an irrational husband thinking he could become superman. Things would be less volatile if she could get him out of the room.

All kinds of thoughts popped into her head. The fact that she was a woman might work to her disadvantage with the gunman. Couldn't be helped. Skill wise, she was better than Reilly and more experienced. She'd have to rely on that.

She went through the checklist one last time.

Don't get shot.

Don't rush.

Do end this peacefully.

Minimal encouragement.

Minimal casualties.

Get the husband out of there first.

Regina was glad she waited. As she was about to stand and approach the conference room door, a voice came over the headset.

"Curry plugged the phone back in. It's live."

Regina's heart skipped a beat in anticipation.

"Patch it through to my headset and dial the number," she said, confidently. Not wanting the team to see the relief that had washed over her. She hadn't looked forward to approaching that door without a gun and no bulletproof vest on.

She heard the sound of the dispatcher dialing the number to the conference room. Then a ringing sound. A bunch of static filled her ear when the ringing stopped.

A weary voice said, "Hello."

"Mr. Curry, my name is Regina Burrows and I'm here to help you today."

"I don't need no help. I know what I aim to do."

She didn't ask him what he aimed to do. No reason to solidify and reaffirm it in his mind. He had already expressed to Leggett that he intended to kill his ex-wife's attorney and himself.

To establish in his mind that there could be a different outcome, she said, "We don't want to see anyone hurt, including you."

"Then do what I say."

She'd remind him later of that promise. If she did what he said, no one would get hurt.

"Can I get you anything?" she asked. "Water. A pizza. Are you hungry Wes?"

Calling him Mr. Curry in the first interaction showed the gunman she respected him. Using his first name now was the first step to building rapport.

The ploy might also work. If he said yes, she could end this thing immediately. All they had to do was spike the water or pizza with a heavy sedative. Curry would take one or two sips or eat a couple of bites of pizza and be out like a light.

She'd successfully used that same tactic many times over the years.

"Nah. I'm good," he answered.

This work required patience. At some point, he'd be hungry or thirsty. At least if she kept him talking long enough.

"What about the people you are holding?" she asked. "Do they need anything?"

"Eve said she needs to use the bathroom, but she'll have to hold it for now."

He used Eve's first name. That's a good thing. It made her personal to him.

"Wes, it's a beautiful day outside, tell me how you got yourself into this situation."

Asking why would be a major blunder. Why questions created defensiveness. Made the gunman think his character was being challenged. Like

Regina was right and he was wrong. How, gave him a chance to explain himself without judgment from her.

"My wife cheated on me."

Before, Curry had been calm. She sensed the first agitation in his voice.

"That woman over there screwed me over," he added.

She assumed he meant the attorney. Pamela Banks.

So far, Curry hadn't cursed. He didn't call the attorney a derogatory name. He used the term "wife" and not any number of vile terms he could've called her.

In the initial briefing, she learned that Curry was a religious man. Regina would use that later. Maybe now. It told her he was conflicted. That good resided deep within him.

"That doesn't sound fair to me," Regina said. "You didn't deserve that."

Her voice had to be sincere and was. If she were to build any level of trust, he had to believe she was genuine. While she knew how to manipulate her own tone to create sincerity, in this case she didn't have to. Perhaps what happened to him wasn't fair.

Her role wasn't priest. Or judge or jury. Her role was to listen and look for an opportunity to end this thing.

"It wasn't fair," he said. "She broke my heart."

"It's not fair that Rich and Eve have to go through this either, is it?"

A long pause developed. Another good thing. Pauses were powerful. She had given him something to think about. Laid the groundwork to get them out.

"Did you know that Rich and Eve have two young kids?" she added.

"Yeah. I know."

"It wouldn't be fair for those kids to grow up without their parents, would it?"

"I ain't doing this for them. I came here to kill Ms. Banks and myself and that's what I intend to do."

"There's no reason to do that. We can work something out. Promise me you won't do anything until we have a chance to talk about it."

He didn't respond. At least her words didn't make him more agitated.

So far, the conversation was going better than normal.

"I want to talk to my wife," he blurted.

The bargaining began. Now she knew what he wanted.

"I can make that happen."

Regina had expected that demand. When she first arrived and learned why the gunman had stormed the offices, she asked the sheriff to track down the ex-wife, just in case. Turned out, the ex was already there. She heard the news reports and came to the law offices immediately upon learning her ex-husband held her attorney hostage.

The ex had demanded to talk to him. Regina wanted to avoid that if possible. In some instances, a spouse could calm an assailant. Perhaps even talk some sense into him. In this case, Regina suspected she'd only make him madder. Remind him why he was there and why he needed to kill her lawyer.

Regina felt her shoulders tense thinking about the news media. She'd seen the satellite trucks when she arrived. Reports through her headset confirmed that the incident had hit the national news. When they learned that the famous lottery winners were two of the hostages.

That meant more scrutiny on her actions. More second guessing if things went bad.

She couldn't let Curry hear the worry in her voice.

"Wes," she said, pausing again. Tonal pacing. "I need you to do something for me."

"I ain't got to do nothing for you. I'm the one with the gun. I'm in charge here. You're going to do what I say, or I'm going to start shooting."

Regina remained calm.

"You aren't going to do that, Wes. I know you don't want to hurt anyone. You only want to talk to your wife. I'm going to make that happen. But you have to do something for me."

"What?"

The response she wanted. It meant he was open to negotiation. They might have a chance of resolving this without anyone getting hurt. At least, she could use his demand to get two of the hostages released.

"I need for you to release Rich and Eve."

She continued to call them by their first names since he had already done so and to make them personal to him. Less likely to kill someone who you are on a first name basis with.

"I already told Rich he could leave. He won't leave without his wife."

"Then let them both go. They haven't done anything to you anyway. This is between you and your wife. I know that you don't want to hurt innocent people."

"No I don't."

"Of course, you don't. I know a lot about you already, Wes. Everybody speaks highly of you. They say you are a good man. I can hear it in your voice."

"I'm not a—," his voice trailed as he cut off his own words. He was obviously riddled with guilt.

She paused to let him finish his thought. When he didn't, she said, "All right. So, we're going to get Rich and Eve out of there. Let's talk about how we can do it without anyone getting hurt."

"How do I know you aren't going to trick me? You're going to shoot me the first chance you get."

Regina heard the first hint of emotion behind his voice. Her words had struck an emotional chord.

"I'm not going to trick you, Wes. We are going to be honest with each other, okay. We aren't going to shoot you. If I say I'm going to do something, I will. I think you'll do the same."

"Then put my wife on the phone."

"I intend to. First, I need you to let Rich and Eve go."

"I want to talk to my wife first."

"I can't do that until you give me something in return. That's how this works. Give and take."

"Then we ain't got a deal. Do you think I'm stupid?"

"Your wife is here. I'll put her on the phone as soon as you let Rich and Eve go."

"She's here!"

Regina heard movement.

Then a gunshot. A flash of light came from inside the conference room.

What the . . .

She heard a blood curdling scream come from inside the room.

"Wes, what happened? Wes, talk to me. Wes, is everyone all right? I heard a gunshot."

Through the headset, she could hear him distressed in the background. His voice was a distance away from the phone.

"Stand by," she told the team, after hitting a switch that let her talk only to them. She switched back in time to hear a frantic Curry.

"No. No. I'm so sorry! The gun went off by mistake."

Regina had to make a decision. Everyone looked at her. SWAT was waiting for her instructions to enter the room. The plan was for them to break the window and throw a flash grenade into the room and enter immediately. With the intent to take down the assailant before he could react. From their vantage point, the SWAT team could get between the assailant and the attorney before he could shoot her.

Curry wouldn't be this distraught unless the bullet had hit someone. Who? The attorney? Rich? Eve?

At that point, she decided to act. Use the distraction to get inside. Before she could give the orders, Curry was back on the phone.

"I didn't mean to do it," he said, practically in tears.

"Do what?" Regina asked.

"The gun went off by mistake. I swear."

"Is someone hurt?"

She could hear the pain in his voice.

"Yes. I shot . . . I shot . . . "

"Who did you shoot?"

"I didn't mean to."

"Wes. Focus. Tell me who you shot."

"Rich. I didn't mean to shoot him."

"Mr. Curry, we need to get medics in there right—"

The line went dead.

13

It seemed to Eve like the nightmare might be coming to an end.

Without warning, the gunman scooted across the floor and reconnected the phone. Within two minutes, the phone rang. Someone on the other line tried to talk some sense into him. That person tried to get Curry to let Rich and her go.

At least, let Rich go. Eve had convinced him he should. For the sake of the kids.

The gunman demanded to speak to his wife. *Ex-wife.* The man was obviously still in denial. From what Eve could tell, Curry and his wife had been divorced for several months now.

Rich was the same way. He kept calling Eve his wife even though they were divorced for all practical purposes. The whole thing was surreal. This was what she wanted, and yet she had regrets. Of course, she did. Who wouldn't. At one time, she was madly in love with Rich.

She blamed the lottery. It changed him. He wasn't the same man she married, which was why they had to get a divorce.

Yet ... was this her fault? She couldn't help but wonder if this whole situation was God's way of punishing her for filing for a divorce. The reality was that they wouldn't be in this predicament had she not done so.

A debate had raged in her head the entire six months. It's like a voice inside of her had been trying to talk her out of divorcing Rich.

Maybe God was trying to protect her from this scenario, and she had been too stubborn to listen.

The debate still bounced around in her head. She had barely slept the night before. If she were honest, she hadn't slept well for six months. The bed seemed cold and empty without Rich in it.

He cheated on me.

That's what she kept telling herself. This wasn't her fault. The Bible was clear. Divorce was allowed in the Bible if your spouse committed adultery.

A tiny voice inside of her head kept disputing that. *Rich didn't cheat on you.*

Yes, he did. I saw what I saw.

Trust God. The two of you can work it out. He still loves you.

She had ignored the voice. Deciding that the enemy was trying to trick her.

Even her mother had joined in the argument.

"You have no proof Rich had sex with any of those women," she said.

"I saw him kiss the nanny."

"You need to forgive him for the sake of the kids."

"You didn't want me to marry him in the first place!"

"And you did anyway. Now you need to make it work."

But she couldn't. She was too hurt.

While she had no real evidence that Rich had sex with any of those women, he certainly acted inappropriately. He had no right not to tell her about the settlements. She was his wife.

Why cover it up if something didn't happen?

That's when she hardened her heart. Which was the cause of divorce according to the Bible. While she needed to forgive Rich, that would have to come later. After the divorce was final. Maybe then she could move on and let the healing process begin.

In the meantime, the bitterness had taken root.

All alone in the middle of the night, she could admit that she was bitter. She had become someone she hated. Which was why she had to get this divorce filed with the court. For her own sanity. So she could move on with her life.

This whole sordid affair was tearing her up inside.

She looked over at Rich who was fixated on the gunman and his conversation. Hope filled his wide eyes.

A feeling of love washed over her. *Where did that come from?* It had warmed her heart when he told the gunman he wasn't leaving without her. He obviously still loved her, and she loved him. Even if she couldn't stay married to him, he'd always have a special place in her heart.

A wave of guilt filled her soul.

Why did she bring up the woman at Peach Ridge? The one Rich helped with the gas containers. Nothing happened with that woman. Rich adored Eve back then. He never would've cheated. She believed his story then and believed it now.

Why did she do that?

To hurt him. Hurt people hurt people. She'd heard that phrase a hundred times.

What she said was cruel.

I'm sorry God.

God get us out of this mess, and I promise I'll forgive Rich.

The prayer sounded desperate and disingenuous in her head. She had to forgive him regardless. That's what the Bible told her to do.

The gunman suddenly got excited and drew her thoughts back to reality.

"She's here!" Eve heard him say. He must be talking about his ex-wife.

Eve looked over at him. The gunman strained to look behind him. Over the conference room table.

Your finger is still on the trigger!

She wanted to shout the words, but everything happened so fast. He had the phone in his left hand and tried to manage the gun with his right.

The gun was pointed right at her.

She tried to let out a scream, but it stuck in her throat. As if she knew what was about to happen.

That's when she heard the loud bang. Saw the blinding flash of light.

Time stood still. It all happened in slow motion.

Sudden movement to her left. *Rich.* Shielding her.

His side was exposed. Toward the gunman.

She heard the sound of a bullet hit flesh. The yelp of pain from Rich.

He exhaled. Their eyes met. His were widened in disbelief.

He slumped into her lap.

She didn't know what to do. Instinctively, she had put her hands in the air to cover her face. Now she put them on Rich. When she put her left hand on his back, his shirt felt wet and sticky. She pulled it back in fear.

That's when she saw the blood and let out a spine-chilling scream.

"No! No! No!" the gunman said frantically. "The gun went off by mistake!"

Rich wasn't moving. She tried to wake him. He was unresponsive.

"I didn't mean to do it," the gunman said into the phone.

"Help him," Eve tried to say, but the words were frozen in the back of her throat.

"The gun went off by mistake," the gunman said to the person on the phone, although he directed it at Eve.

"You shot him!" Eve shouted, through her dry mouth. "You have to help him. He's dying."

"The gun went off by mistake, I swear."

"I don't care. We need help. Tell them to call an ambulance."

He ignored her.

"Yes. I shot ... I shot."

"Tell them you shot Rich. He needs help."

He hesitated. Frozen in place.

Tears streamed down her face now. She reached to wipe them away and felt the sticky blood on her fingers, now smeared on her cheeks.

Eve was sobbing now. She pulled Rich close to her. His body felt lifeless.

"Help him!" she cried out. "He's going to die."

The gunman ignored her, so she talked to Rich.

"You can't die. Our kids need you."

"I didn't mean to," the gunman said to the person on the phone.

"Tell her you shot Rich!" Eve demanded.

"Rich," he said into the phone. "I didn't mean to."

That's when he slammed the phone down on the hook.

"Are they coming?" Eve said.

"I don't know."

"You have to help him," Eve said. "You can't let him die."

The gunman put his back against the conference table. His eyes were crazed with confusion. Darting back and forth. Pamela Banks sat in the corner and shivered in fear.

For a moment, Eve thought he was going to shoot her. He pointed the gun at her, then grimaced. Pulled the gun back and put his head in his hand.

"What have I done?" he said. "What have I done?"

He rocked back and forth like a child.

The phone rang.

"Answer it," Eve demanded.

He hesitated again.

"Answer it! Or I will."

He picked up the phone. "Yeah."

Eve stroked Rich's hair to try to rouse him. He wasn't moving. She feared the worst. He was dead. Or dying. If they didn't get help for him soon, it'd be too late.

"I'll let the medics in," she heard the gunman say. "But don't try anything. You can take him to the hospital. That's it. Give me one minute."

Eve wasn't sure Rich had a minute.

Moving him didn't seem like a good idea so she left him on her lap and waited. Curry hung up the phone and jumped to his feet. The conference table looked heavy, but he easily slid it across the carpet and away from the door.

He cautiously unlocked the door. Vaulted over the conference room table to get to the other side of the room where Banks was standing now.

She let out a shriek when he grabbed her and held her in front of him as a human shield. He had the gun pointed at the door.

"Is it okay to enter?" Eve heard a voice at the door say.

"Yeah. But no funny business."

The door opened and a woman wearing a headset entered first. She held out her hands in a form of surrender.

"I'm not armed," she said. "I'm Regina. The woman you've been talking to."

"I didn't mean to shoot him."

"I know."

Once the woman signaled for the medics to enter, they were by Rich's side within seconds. They didn't move him right away. The EMT checked for a pulse. Eve saw the concern flash across his face when it formed a grimace. Confirmed when he shook his head to the other EMT with him.

"I don't get a pulse," he said.

"He was shot in the side," Eve said. "Under his left arm. The bullet was headed toward me. He put himself in the way of the bullet."

They carefully lifted Rich's head off of Eve, sat him on the floor, and examined the wound on his back. One EMT covered the wound with her hand and pressed hard while the other performed CPR.

Eve scooted away to give them room.

Another set of EMT's entered the room with a stretcher. They had to move the conference table in order to get in completely.

"Is he going to live?" Curry asked with what seemed like genuine concern.

They didn't answer.

"Let's hope so," Regina said. "All we can do is pray that he does."

The EMT continued CPR for what seemed like an eternity but was only about two minutes. Another EMT hooked up an IV to Rich's arm.

"He has a pulse, but it's faint," one of them said.

"Let's move."

They lifted Rich onto the stretcher. The white carpet where he'd been lying had turned red. Eve stood to her feet. She retrieved her purse off the floor and had the presence of mind to grab the divorce papers as well and stuff them into her purse.

"I didn't say you could go," Curry said roughly.

"You'll have to shoot me to stop me," Eve said. "I'm going, and you can't stop me."

"Let her go be with her husband," Regina said calmly.

Before Curry could respond, the EMT's were out the door and so was Eve. The law office was on the fourth floor, and it took almost a minute for the elevator to arrive and for them to get to the street level.

As they prepared to load Rich into the ambulance, the driver asked Eve, "Are you a family member?"

"I'm his wife."

"You can ride up front with me."

"I'd like to be with my husband."

"It's not allowed."

Eve didn't want to waste time arguing. Rich was already inside the ambulance, and they were only waiting for the driver. The EMT's were still furiously working on Rich. It'd be better if she weren't in the way.

The drive took less than five minutes. Someone must've called ahead because a team of nurses and doctors were outside the emergency room entrance waiting for them.

Rich was out of the back and into the hospital almost as quickly as Eve could exit the vehicle. As she followed them in, she was stopped by a woman who requested information. Rich's name, social security number, age, address, phone number, allergies to medications. Those kinds of things.

Before Eve could finish the paperwork, a doctor appeared.

"Mrs. Martin," she said.

"Yes."

"Your husband is being taken back to surgery."

"How is he?"

"I won't lie to you. It's not good. He's lost a lot of blood, and the bullet collapsed his lungs and has done extensive damage to some of his internal organs. We won't know how much damage until we get in there. I would suggest that you call his closest friends and relatives who would want to be here."

Eve remembered the kids at home with a sitter. She'd have to make arrangements for someone to watch them. She didn't want them brought there. The media had already filled up the emergency room and were snapping pictures of her.

The doctor pulled Eve to the side. "Is there someone who could bring you a set of clothes," she whispered.

"Um."

Eve looked down at her clothes which were stained with blood. Her hands were sticky and red.

"You have blood on your face," the doctor said. "Here, come with me."

She led Eve through the double doors and back to the emergency room area. To a restroom. "You can get cleaned up in here. I'm going to bring you some scrubs to wear until you can get some new clothes."

When Eve looked in the mirror, she couldn't believe what she saw. Her face and hair were stained with a mixture of blood and tears. Her eyes had dark bags under them. She barely recognized who she had become.

The last six months had taken a bigger toll than she realized. The last few hours had drained her face of life.

The next six hours were a whirlwind. The police arrived to interview her. She told them what she knew. They also formed a huge presence both inside and outside the hospital, took control of the news media, and isolated them a distance away from her outside the hospital so she'd have some privacy.

The lady who had entered the conference room wearing the headset showed up a couple hours later. Eve learned that she was the hostage negotiator.

"What happened to Pamela?" Eve asked.

"The gunman surrendered. He's in custody. She's shaken up, but unharmed from what I can tell."

Eve was relieved to hear those words.

"Thank you for all you did to get us out of there."

"I wish I could've done more. Without anyone getting hurt." Her voice trailed off as she said the last words. "How is Mr. Martin?"

"He's in surgery. I haven't heard."

Eve looked at the clock on the wall. Rich had been in surgery for more than three hours.

By that time, literally hundreds of people from the church had arrived and filled up the emergency room. Eve went to thank them.

"We've set up a prayer chain," Ben, the chairman of the elders, said. He was acting pastor until they found someone and had been for the past six months. Ever since Rich resigned.

"Thank you."

"You and Rich are loved," he said. "You need to know that."

"I do know that."

"We're your family. And we're here for you."

Several of Eve's closest friends from church were allowed back to wait with her. They brought her a change of clothes, and she was able to shower in the room and get cleaned up.

Rich was in surgery for more than seven hours. The wait was excruciating. She wanted the surgeon to show up at the door but was afraid of what he might say when he did.

Her heart skipped a couple of beats when he finally stepped into the private waiting room. His eyebrows were furrowed in deep concern.

"Rich is stable. For the moment. The surgery went about as well as could be expected. The bullet collapsed his lungs, then bounced off a rib and settled against his spine. We weren't able to remove it."

"What does that mean?"

"We don't know. Your husband was brought back from the dead three times. Once by the EMT's, again in the emergency room, and then on the operating table. He may have suffered brain damage. He may have suffered spinal cord damage. We just won't know until he wakes up."

"Will he wake up?"

"It's touch and go. Your husband is in critical condition. The good thing is that he's breathing on his own. Even with the damage to his lungs That's a minor miracle. He's also young and strong. He obviously has something to live for."

"There are a lot of people praying."

"Keep it up. The prayers are working. Your husband should really not be alive right now."

After he left, Eve went and informed all the members of the church still congregated in the lobby. Outside the hospital, the doctors briefed the media.

Rich was brought to a room in the ICU. Eve was the only one allowed in to see him. Her heart broke when she saw him lying there hooked up to all the machines. In a coma.

The lights were dimmed. Nighttime had fallen. The only sound in the room was the steady beeping of the heart monitor and the frequent sound of the blood pressure machine which came on every few minutes.

Eve pulled her chair close to the bed and took Rich's hand.

An intense feeling of love for him overwhelmed her.

Tears streamed down her face. She didn't want to release his hand to wipe them away, so she didn't.

"Why did you put yourself in front of that bullet?" she asked. "You must love me or something."

Why had she doubted that?

"How did we get to this place, Rich?"

She paused as if he could answer.

The tears blurred her vision. She buried her head in the hospital bedspread. Still clutching Rich's hand.

"I never stopped loving you," she said, not bothering to choke back the tears. "I'm sorry I was so mean."

She looked over at her purse on the table. The divorce papers were still in there. The still, small voice that had been hounding her for months started another conversation with her.

The divorce isn't final.

"It's too late," Eve said.

With God, all things are possible.

"The papers are signed."

A Bible verse popped into her mind. First Peter 5:10. *The God of grace, who called you to his eternal glory in Christ, after you have suffered a little while, will himself restore you and make you strong, firm, and steadfast.*

I can restore your marriage.

"The doctor said that Rich might die," she whispered to God. "He might have brain damage. He might not ever walk again."

I can make him strong, firm, and steadfast again.

"How do I know Rich even wants to be with me? After all I said to him."

No greater love has a man, than to lay down his life.

"God, is it really you talking to me?"

My sheep hear my voice.

"Did Rich have sex with any of those women?" Why did she ask that? Why was she so obsessed with the settlements and the women? What if Rich had been telling the truth all along? She'd feel like a fool.

But she had to ask. Had to know.

No. The still small voice answered clearly and emphatically.

"Did he want to?"

No.

"So, he was telling the truth?"

He loves you. What I have brought together, don't let any man tear apart.

"I don't want to lose him."

She couldn't believe the words coming out of her mouth. The settlements didn't matter now.

You don't have to.

Doubt came back with a vengeance.

"Will he cheat on me in the future?"

I'm not going to answer that.

"Why not?" she said angrily. "I deserve to know."

Love always trusts. Always believes. Always hopes. Always perseveres.

"So, I have to trust him?"

You should trust me. I brought you together. I can sustain you.

For whatever reason, she believed the voice. Believed Rich over the women.

She stood to her feet and walked over to her purse. Took out the divorce papers and stared at them. Flipped to the back and looked at the signatures. Tears dripped down her face and wet the papers.

For the next thirty minutes, she begged God to save Rich and bring him back to her. Not sure what she would do with those papers if he did.

At some point, her heart completely softened and turned back to her husband.

"I promise, God," Eve said, "if you'll save my husband, I will love him with all my heart for the rest of our lives. If he'll have me."

The voice only said one more thing.

Only three things remain. Faith, hope, and love. The greatest of these is love.

With resolve, Eve ripped up the divorce papers. Tore them into several pieces and threw them in the trash can next to the hospital bed.

She walked back over to Rich and gently kissed his lips. Then whispered in his ear.

"I'm here, honey," she said. "I'll never leave you. Come back to me. Things will be different, I promise."

14

"We have two special guests here today," Ben said to the roughly fifteen-hundred people in the sanctuary that morning.

Attendance was up slightly, probably because word had gotten out to a limited number of people that Rich and Eve were the special guests.

"Today's service is going to be a little different than most. We have been praying for this couple fervently over the last three weeks. I'm pleased to inform you that Pastor Rich is out of the hospital. He was discharged yesterday. And he's here with us today."

Applause rippled through the sanctuary, then picked up steam until everyone was clapping.

"Pastor Rich asked me if he could come and say a few words and thank everyone personally for their prayers. I said of course. We wouldn't have this building, and this church wouldn't exist without his hard work and his generosity. Will you put your hands together for Pastor Rich and his wife Eve?"

Rich and Eve were standing off to the side backstage. Rich walked with a cane, and Eve had to help him to the podium. A stool was in place for him, but he wanted to stand.

For the first time in six months, he looked out over the congregation he loved. The last time he stood in that spot was when he resigned in disgrace.

He felt pain in his heart because the church was half empty. He hadn't seen that few people in the sanctuary since they started. Before everything came crashing in around him, *Life Church* had three full services a week.

Not only was the sanctuary half-full; this one was the only service left of the three.

Nevertheless, the applause was enthusiastic which warmed his aching heart. Several people suddenly stood. Before long everyone stood and cheered.

His eyes filled with tears. He said a silent prayer that God would give him the strength and the right words.

The doctor had advised against him speaking that morning. Rich ignored it. He felt like the Holy Spirit was leading him.

"Thank you," he said several times. "Please, be seated. Thank you."

Eve held his arm tightly, otherwise, he might've fallen down as his knees felt weak from standing for that long backstage.

"Four days ago," Rich said, starting his words slowly and solemnly, "I woke up from a coma. When I opened my eyes, the first thing I saw was this lovely lady next to me. I'm told she had been at my bedside the entire three weeks. Only leaving long enough to spend time with our kids. I'm so thankful for her."

The audience stood again, applauding enthusiastically. Rich looked over and saw Eve blush.

He felt strength build in his body and in his spirit.

"The first thing I said when I saw her was 'Am I in heaven?'" He laughed.

"She told me I was in the hospital. 'Why do you think you're in heaven?' she asked me. I said, 'Because you look like an angel.'"

Everyone roared and Eve blushed some more.

Rich waited for them to quiet down.

He continued. "The doctor said I died three times. He told Eve I had less than a ten-percent chance of making it. If I did somehow survive, I might wake up brain damaged. Eve told the doctor that I was already a little brain damaged anyway, so she probably wouldn't notice."

Eve slapped Rich on the chest and leaned into the microphone. "I did not say that."

"The doctor said I would probably never walk again. Obviously, the doctor didn't know my God."

The people stood and applauded. Giving thanks to the Lord. This time, they stayed on their feet.

"He also didn't know about all y'all. Or about the power of prayer. About the spiritual law of agreement. I'm told that this church had an around-the-clock prayer chain going for me. Every hour of every day, someone was praying for me. Sometimes more than one person. I can tell you that the reason I'm here today is because of the love of a woman and the prayers of this church."

The crowd erupted in cheers. Whooping and hollering. Raising the rafters. Rich had never heard it that loud. Even when the place was full.

He looked at the camera in the back of the room fixed on him. The services were still broadcast live. Rich had continued to support the finances of the church even though he was no longer pastor and had insisted they continue broadcasting the services.

"I'm alive because I have something to live for," Rich said. He looked at Eve, who smiled meekly. Tears had filled her eyes. "And because God is not through with me yet."

More applause.

"It's a miracle that I'm alive," Rich said. "But I want to tell you about a greater miracle. God has used this horrible tragedy to save our marriage."

Everyone burst into applause.

"You may or may not know this, but the reason Eve and I were at those law offices that day was to sign divorce papers. In fact, they were already signed."

He paused to let that sink in.

"If that gunman hadn't barged in when he did, our divorce would already be final. Now, I'm not saying God sent the gunman. What I'm saying is that God can use anything for good."

The crowd roared in agreement.

"Regardless, I'm thankful. God has given me back my bride. My soulmate. The love of my life."

Rich put his arm around Eve. She pressed her head onto his shoulder. The crowd shouted encouragement.

"Can I say something?" she whispered to Rich.

"Of course," he said. He moved to the side, and she took his spot in front of the microphone. The sanctuary got so quiet you could almost hear a car drive by outside.

"I want to thank everyone as well," Eve said. "Thank you. I love you so much. Everyone was so supportive when Rich was in the hospital. You brought us meals. Helped care for my kids. I'm so thankful."

She was interrupted by more applause. It died down quickly. The people hung on to her every word. With rapt attention.

"When Rich was lying in that hospital bed, dying, I had a come-to-Jesus moment. I saw my life and I didn't like who I had become. I was filled with bitterness and anger. Unforgiveness."

She fought back tears. Rich could tell she was trying to hold it together. It took all his strength to stand, since she no longer held onto his arm.

"I want to apologize publicly to you, Rich, and to all of you. We let you down. We didn't lead you well. We were not a good example for you."

"We forgive you," someone shouted.

She smiled sheepishly.

"Thank you. In that hospital room, not knowing if Rich was going to live or die, I heard the Lord's voice. Not audibly. But that still, small voice. It had been there all along, but I ignored it for so many months. The Holy Spirit told me to trust my husband. He said that I didn't have to go through with that divorce. He told me that my husband didn't cheat on me with those women. I know that now. He never should've had to resign from the church. That's my fault. Because of me, you all believed the worst in him. I hope you will forgive me. And not blame Rich for my weaknesses."

Eve began to cry.

"I feel so badly about everything that happened," she said. "I'm so thankful to Rich for forgiving me. Thankful to God that he restored our marriage before it was too late."

Rich pulled her close. This wasn't the first time they'd had a moment like this. The main time was in the hospital room when he first opened his eyes and saw her there. She told him she had torn up the divorce papers.

He was thrilled even in his fragile state. He could tell God was doing something special in Eve. And in him.

Eve was finished talking, so Rich said, "I want to ask your forgiveness as well. I didn't act inappropriately with those women, but I did a lot of things to let you down. When we won the lottery, I thought all our problems were over. That we could use the money for good. Like God needs our money. He doesn't. Never did. Don't get me wrong, a lot of good did come from it. I'm proud of all that we accomplished. Mostly, I'm thrilled by all the people who we've touched through this ministry. All of you who helped make all this possible."

He waited for them to applaud, then continued.

"I have a confession to make to you as well. At some point, it all went to my head. The money. The fame. The applause. Being on television. I thought I had arrived. That it was more about me than it was about God. I thought the reason thousands were flocking to my church ... our church. See what I mean. I used to call it *my* church. It's not mine. It belongs to God. It belongs to you."

Rich pointed at the cameras when he said it.

"I was famous. My head got so big, it barely fit inside this building."

Everyone laughed.

"I began neglecting my family and my kids. I bought five sports cars. Why would I do that? To feed my ego which was getting bigger by the day. That's why I hid the settlements with those women. I didn't want to lose all this. I was afraid. So, I hid it from my wife and from all of you. You deserved better than that. The Scripture says man likes to keep things in the dark that are evil. Things like that should be brought into the light. Will you forgive me?"

"We forgive you!" several people shouted, and the chorus joined them.

"Thank you. It means the world to me and Eve. And I want to tell you that God is going to use me again. I believe that. He has restored my marriage and someday, he'll let me pastor again."

"Why can't it be here?" someone shouted. "We want you to be our pastor!"

The entire room began chanting. "Rich! Rich! Rich!"

He didn't know what to say.

Ben approached the microphone and said, "It sounds like you want Rich to come back and lead us."

A resounding cheer echoed through the room.

"That's fine by me," Ben said. "I'm not a pastor. I've been trying to hold it together. I could never lead us like Rich did."

"We want Rich!"

Rich could hardly believe it.

"All in favor, say aye," Ben said.

The whole room said aye.

"Any opposed, say no!"

One person in the back of the sanctuary shouted, "No!"

Everyone groaned and turned to look.

Rich shielded his eyes from the bright lights beating down on the stage. He looked in the direction the familiar voice had come from. As he suspected, standing in the back was Mrs. Ballard, from Peach Ridge Community Church. The woman who led the charge to have him fired from the first church. The one he suspected was the lone dissenting vote there as well.

Rich laughed when he saw her. She must've seen him on television and came to stick her nose in things and get some gossip to take back to her ladies.

"That's the second time you were the only one who voted against me," Rich said.

"Who is that?" Ben asked, turning his head away from the microphone so only Rich could hear.

"I'll tell you later."

"According to my count, the ayes have it," Ben said, speaking directly into the microphone. "Let me be the first to welcome you back to the pulpit, Rich."

"Thank you. And I accept. Do you mind if I preach the sermon this morning?" Rich asked.

The Holy Spirit had come upon him strongly and given him a word.

"Do you think you should?" Eve asked.

"It's okay," Rich said. "I'll be fine."

Eve reluctantly left the stage and sat down in the first row. Rich used the cane to hold himself up. For whatever reason, the church's faith in him had emboldened him, and he felt stronger.

Forty minutes later, Rich was still going. With increased vigor. Getting stronger with each word. At some point, he had discarded the cane without even realizing it. He also noticed that the building had more people in it than when he started the sermon. They were obviously watching television and wanted to see it in person.

At exactly the forty-minute mark, Rich felt the Holy Spirit descend on him with power like he had never felt before. Instructing him to do something unusual.

He hesitated.

The service had already gone too long. But the urge was overwhelming. So, he qualified it, "I feel led that we aren't supposed to end this service. Not yet. However, I know it's late. If you need to leave, feel free. If you have kids in the nursery or in the kid's service, please go get them. We don't want to burden our workers. Feel free to bring them into this service if you want. That's fine. We're going to continue for a while."

He waited as a few hundred people left. A few hundred more entered the sanctuary shortly thereafter. Within seconds, the sanctuary was almost full.

"The Bible says to confess your sins, one to another so that you may be healed," Rich said, repeating the words he felt like the Lord had put in his mind. "When I came face to face with how I had wronged Eve and wronged you and confessed it, that's when healing came."

He stepped out from behind the podium.

"Did you notice that I don't need my cane? That God has healed me? I feel as strong as I did before the shooting."

He began to walk with a purpose back and forth on the stage to demonstrate it to them. He had to silence them when the applause went on too long.

"I feel like I'm supposed to give this time to you. Like I said, this isn't my church. This is your church. This is God's church. It's not all about me. Ben, can you get me a handheld microphone?"

Rich left the stage and walked down the steps to the front of the auditorium. Ben was waiting and handed him a microphone.

"If you have something you want to share with everyone, this is your time. Come and get in line right over here."

He pointed to his right.

At first, no one moved. Rich wondered if he had actually heard from God. He waited. Confident that the Lord had told him what to do.

Someone stood. A woman. Then a man. That's all it took. Before the first person made it to the microphone, a dozen people were in line.

For two hours, people came forward and shared. Some confessed hidden sins. Some apologized to their husband or wife. Rich saw marriages restored right before his eyes.

Some came for physical healing. Emotional problems. One man was an alcoholic. Another addicted to drugs. One had lost his job and was about to lose his house. A businessman confessed to filing false tax returns.

Rich had them turn off the television cameras because of the sensitive nature of what people were sharing. He didn't sense judgment in the room. He only sensed love. He asked anyone who felt led to come and pray with someone to do so.

He almost fell over when he saw the next person in line.

He hadn't seen her come forward. He didn't think she was still at the church. She might not have been. The entire sanctuary was completely full, and people stood in the back and in the aisles. She might've seen what was happening on television and came there. Compelled to speak.

What was she going to say? He could see her ruining everything God was doing.

"Hello, Emily," Rich said as he reluctantly handed her the microphone. Then instinctively took two steps back.

Emily was practically sobbing. She bit her lip trying to choke back the tears.

"I'm Emily. I'm one of the girls who got ten thousand dollars," she said. Her voice cracked. "I have a confession to make."

She broke down and buried her head in her hands. Eve sat in the front row and was by her side in a second.

"I'm so sorry, Mrs. Martin," Emily said. "I lied. Your husband was always a perfect gentleman around me. I did it for the money. All of us did."

Eve put her arm around the young girl.

She continued with more resolve. "Word had gotten around that we could get money from Pastor Rich if we made up a story."

The elders had suspected as much. The stories had sounded similar, and the timing was suspect. No one ever corroborated their stories.

"Will you forgive me?" Emily said to Eve.

"Of course, I will, honey."

"Jackie was lying too."

Jackie was their nanny. The one who kissed Rich and got $75,000.

"She's my cousin. I'm so ashamed. I ... I ... told her that you were looking for a nanny. That's why she applied. She only did it so she could get money from you. I'm sorry."

Eve looked at Rich. As if to offer her own apology for not believing him. That water was long under the bridge.

This became a teaching moment for Rich. He stood in front of Eve and Emily. Keeping a distance but close enough to look her in the eyes.

"There is no condemnation to those in Christ Jesus. He took our shame, the Bible says. God forgives you and so do we."

He turned back around. "This is another miracle. God is moving and restoring relationships. He's freeing us from guilt, shame, and condemnation!"

Eve led Emily to the side and several of the ladies surrounded her and began to pray for her.

Rich's heart skipped a beat when he saw who entered the back of the sanctuary.

Wes Curry. The gunman.

What's he doing here? Rich had heard he was out on bail. With orders not to come within five hundred yards of Rich, Eve, Pamela Banks, his ex-wife, or the law offices.

Curry walked down the aisle and got in the back of the line. Rich wanted to alert security, but the next person already had the microphone.

If Curry had a weapon, he'd hidden it in the back of his pants.

Peace suddenly came over Rich and he wasn't afraid. Maybe God was doing a work in Curry's heart as well. His turn came and he took the microphone from Rich.

The entire room collectively gasped when they saw him and immediately recognized the man whose face had been all over the television.

Curry chuckled nervously. "Don't worry. I'm not going to hurt anyone. For those of you who don't know, I'm the one who shot Pastor Rich. He never did nothing to me. I didn't mean to, but it was still my fault."

He shuffled his feet and looked down. Rich put his hand on Curry's shoulder.

"I know that I have no right to ask," he said, "but will you forgive me, Pastor?"

"I already have," Rich said. "And God forgives you as well."

Curry handed Rich the microphone. Rich took it, then held out his arms. Curry took him into a bear hug and sobbed in his arms.

That's when Rich realized God had completely healed his wounds. Curry was a massive man and was squeezing him. It didn't hurt at all.

The service went until midnight. Rich could've gone all night.

"We're going to call it a night," he said to a loud groan. "But we'll meet back here at ten o'clock tomorrow. And we'll do it over again. We'll do this every day until the Lord tells us to stop."

They didn't stop for seven years.

15

The media named what happened in southern Georgia, *The Lottery Revival*. The term was meant to be disparaging, but Rich liked it. In looking back, he could see God's hand in everything. Winning the lottery had been part of God's plan. Not so he could own five sports cars and a beach house. But so they could build that facility. Have the resources to handle what was to come so unexpectedly.

Over the seven years, 7.5 million people visited the revival from around the world. More than half a million people were baptized and more than a million were saved.

The services took place every week, Tuesday through Sunday. Monday was set aside for prayer. The services started at ten in the morning and went until they were over. Usually around midnight although they often went through the night.

Logistics should've been a problem but weren't. God provided hundreds of volunteers. Many musicians and worship leaders. Dozens of pastors spoke. Rich spoke almost every day.

A lot of time was spent with an open microphone. Like it started. People shared their hearts. Confessed their sins one to another. Got right with God.

The revival spread. Churches around the country began to experience the same move of God. Literally thousands of pastors visited Peach Ridge to get ideas. That's why Rich eventually decided to end the services. Not because interest waned, but because he wanted people to know that they could experience the same thing at their own churches.

People wanted to meet him. To be baptized by him. While he was touched, he was concerned that they might be seeking a man and not God. They didn't have to come to Georgia to be healed or to meet God.

So, he started a school of ministry, trained pastors and sent them around the world to start churches. Tuition was free. The lottery money provided funding to start churches around the world.

Also, prison ministries.

Wes Curry was sentenced to thirty years in prison. Almost immediately, he started a ministry in his prison. Wes was on fire for God, and the revival had spread to the facility. So much so that over the seven years, the prison population in that penitentiary had been cut by a third.

Rich remembered reading that during the Welsh revival back in the 1800s, all the prisons were empty because no one committed crimes. Most of the criminals had given their hearts to Jesus.

Wes's first parole hearing was in a couple of years. Rich wanted to come and testify on his behalf. Wes wouldn't let him.

"I'm doing too much good here. This is my purpose in life. I want to stay."

Rich left his attorney's office and headed home. As usual, Eve was at the door to greet him with a huge kiss.

"How did it go?" Eve asked, after he had a chance to settle in from the long day.

"Good. The foundation is in place now."

The rest of their lottery money was put into a foundation. Run by a board of directors. To be invested wisely. That'd guarantee that the work they had started would continue for years to come and after they were gone.

"That's awesome. I'm so proud of you," Eve said. "That makes me happy that the money is going to be put to good use."

Rich had sold all five of his sports cars. They had two SUV's now. Which they needed since Eve gave birth to two more kids during the seven years.

Rich sat down in his favorite chair, and Eve came and sat on his lap. She put both arms around his neck. The lavender scent in her hair tickled his nose and warmed his heart.

"I did something else today," Rich said. "You won 't believe it."

"What?"

"Mrs. Ballard turned one hundred today. I sent her flowers."

"Shut the front door!"

"I did. I wished her a happy birthday. The Bible says to love those who persecute you."

"I can't believe she's still alive."

"She is."

"Well, I'm proud of you for taking the high road."

"The delivery man said she took one look at the card and smashed the vase and flowers on the ground. Slammed the door behind her."

"I guess there are some things money can't buy. Like Mrs. Ballard's approval."

"Yes, there are."

"Like me. Money can't buy me."

"I don't know about that."

"Rich Martin! What are you talking about? You can't buy my affection."

"Yes, I can."

"No, you cannot."

Rich reached into his pants pocket and pulled out two candy bars and flashed them before her.

Her smile widened. "Oh. I want those."

"You can have them for a kiss."

Without hesitation, she planted a big kiss on his lips.

"See, I was right," Rich said. "I can buy your affection."

She snatched the two candy bars out of his hands.

"Meet me in the bedroom. I'll show you what two chocolate bars can get you."

He was out of his chair before she finished the words.

I've got the best life.

He couldn't believe how close he came to losing it. Eve was right. The largest lottery jackpot in the world can't buy happiness, but it can take it away from you if you let it.

Something he knew all too well.

Thank God it didn't.

The End

Thank you for purchasing this novel from best-selling author, Terry Toler. As an additional thank you, Terry wants to give you a free gift.

Sign up for:

Updates

New Releases

Announcements

At terrytoler.com

We'll send you an eBook, *The Book Club*, a Cliff Hangers novella, free of charge.

READ MORE BOOKS FROM TERRY TOLER

Jamie Austen Thrillers

Read all the Jamie Austen Thrillers. They must be good.
They've been number one on Amazon in ten different countries.
Click on the link below.

THE JAMIE AUSTEN THRILLERS (12 book series)
Kindle Edition (amazon.com)

https://amzn.to/3vmPUy7

Cliff Hangers Mystery Series

Who wants to read a good mystery? We've got you covered! Read the Cliff Hangers where homicide detective, Cliff Ford, solves crimes in Chicago, with help from his wife Julia. These books have everything Terry Toler is known for. Page turning suspense, a hint of romance, and an ending you won't see coming.

The Cliff Hangers Mystery Series (4 book series)
Kindle Edition (amazon.com)

https://amzn.to/36WX3go

About Terry

Terry Toler is an Amazon international # 1 best-selling and award-winning author. He writes clean fiction with a message and life-changing nonfiction. He's a public speaker, entrepreneur, and has authored more than forty books.

Sign up for his newsletter where you'll get free stuff, exclusive content, and news of releases and promotions. He can be followed at terrytoler.com.

If you like his books, please take a few minutes to leave a review on Amazon. We really appreciate it. It helps draw more readers to his books. Thanks!